P9-EFI-476

THE BUTLER GETS A BREAK

a Bellweather Tale

KRISTIN CLARK VENUTI

EGMONT
USA

NEW YORK

EGMONT

We bring stories to life

First published by Egmont USA, 2010
443 Park Avenue South, Suite 806
New York, NY 10016

1 3 5 7 9 8 6 4 2

www.egmontusa.com
www.leavingthebellweathers.com

Library of Congress Cataloging-in-Publication Data

Venuti, Kristin Clark.
The butler gets a break : a Bellweather tale / Kristin Clark Venuti.
p. cm.
Summary: Having published his tell-all memoir, put-upon
butler Tristan Benway returns to work for the eccentric
Bellweather family at Eel-Smack-by-the-Bay, only to break
his leg when the triplets destroy the lighthouse stairs.
ISBN 978-1-60684-087-0
[1. Household employees—Fiction. 2. Eccentrics and eccentricities—Fiction.
3. Family life—Fiction. 4. Authorship—Fiction.
5. Lighthouses—Fiction. 6. Humorous stories.] I. Title.
PZ7.V57But 2010
[Fic]—dc22
2010022141

Printed in the United States of America

CPSIA tracking label information:
Random House Production • 1745 Broadway • New York, NY 10019

For the Usual Suspects

And for my
dear friend and
writing mentor,
Kevin McCaughey.
Thank you for
encouraging my closer
acquaintance with the
Bellweathers when
I (being sane) would
have otherwise run
from them.

Contents

THE BUTLER GETS A BREAK

In the village of Eel-Smack-by-the-Bay there stands a lighthouse on a hill, known to residents as the Lighthouse on the Hill. Inside that structure resides the most chaotic family ever to live. And their butler. And sometimes endangered animals that have the ability to poison, maim, or kill in a gruesome manner. And sometimes hobos. And sometimes famous works of art that have been Anonymously Borrowed.*

As always, if one is brave enough to get close to the

* See *Leaving the Bellweathers*, the first book in the Bellweather ordeal . . . er . . . saga.

Lighthouse on the Hill, one can look up into the third-story window and see an upright man, at an upright desk, up writing in his diary.

July 7

Dear Journal,

Just now, when I penned the above date (in this Most Excellent Penmanship, which I inherited from my great-great-great-great-grandfather) I was struck by the fact that on this day one year ago, I was counting down the weeks (and indeed, the days, hours, and minutes) until I could escape my Life of Servitude as butler to the most chaotic family ever to live in a lighthouse.

I planned to leave the village of Eel-Smack-by-the-Bay entirely and retire to a quiet Cottage Far, Far Away.

Alas, I was prevented from doing so by the terms of "The Benway Family Oath of Fealty" made by my ancestor to theirs . . . and by a certain lack of funds for retirement. The publication of my memoir (I dislike the term "tell-all book") is helping a little in that direction. Still, I now feel myself to be bound to the family by something else. Something I feel no need to get into at the present. A year ago I was a bit put out. Not that I would ever have displayed such emotion. Certainly not! To do so would have been unprofessional, and I did, after all, graduate first in my class from the B. Knighted Academy for Butlers. In my own defense, anyone would be put out by having to share living quarters with an Endangered Albino Alligator brought into the home by a fourteen-year-old boy. The same goes for having to put up with a thirteen-year-old girl who ~~kidnaps~~ hides a family of circus performers and their pet seal in her bedroom for weeks on end. Finally, I defy anyone to not React Badly when they discover that nine-year-old triplets have stolen the Mona Lisa.

Blessedly, that is all in the past and I do fancy that it was I who helped them to see the errors of their ways.

There remains the matter of the small, vicious beasts that Spider smuggled into Eel-Smack years ago. The disaster that resulted is partly my fault, though Spider is unaware of my involvement in the case. He believes that the squirrels escaped, when the truth is, I let them go. They were messy and bad tempered and there were too many (an even dozen) to be kept in the boy's bedroom lair.

The liberation took place three years ago.

I am afraid that for an endangered species they have managed to increase their population at a Rather Alarming rate.

On afternoons off, it is my custom to capture and deposit them far from Eel-Smack-by-the-Bay. I see no need to let Spider know this. While I generally believe in taking responsibility for any mistakes that are made, I fear that doing so in this case might encourage him to commit other unwise acts.

Oh, I am not claiming that they are saints. Still, the children's messes aren't nearly as bad as the ones they created before. Now when they see I have helped them, they are oh so careful to thank me. This makes all the difference.

Recently for instance, Ninda had a bit of trouble with the mayor of Eel-Smack-by-the-Bay. He'd just had a swimming pool installed at the taxpayers' expense and was threatening to close the public library in order to balance the budget. She, her favorite librarian, and some other concerned citizens littered the front lawn of the mayoral mansion with bread as a symbol of the money he'd wasted. The protesters were chased off the property, and I was forced to hide a group of them in my living quarters for several hours. After they left, Ninda expressed her gratitude by mopping the circular staircase that winds up through the middle of the lighthouse from Spider's basement lair to the seventh-floor observation deck.

While I was thankful for her gratitude, there is the uncomfortable fact that she has taken me on as a project, dedicating herself to my comfort and education in human rights. I would say that her attentions have become trying except that they've been that way all along.

I must say I am most pleased with the reformation of the triplets. For a year now, I've not had to clean up a single mess made by Spike, Brick, and Sassy. I am Quite Confident that they are no longer engaging in the unholy destruction they refer to as ART.

• 1 •
The Butler Is Mistaken

The sun was just peeping over the horizon when the triplets awakened and crept downstairs to prepare their favorite breakfast, bananas and gravy.

Anyone who is familiar with twins or triplets knows that while there might be strong similarities in appearance, one can usually tell the individuals apart by some difference in behavior. For instance, Brick Bellweather speaks in a Very Loud Voice, loves strange food combinations, and has an intense desire to make the world Sit Up and Take Notice. Spike Bellweather loves strange food combinations, has an intense desire to make the world Sit Up and Take Notice, and speaks in a Very Loud Voice. Sassy Bellweather has an intense desire to make the world Sit Up and Take Notice, speaks in a Very Loud Voice, and loves strange food combinations.

The three never communicate at a decibel below earsplitting, unless they are Up to No Good. Then they whisper. When *that* happens, hairs on the necks of humans and animals alike stand on end, for near disaster always follows in the wake of that terrible, terrible sound.

The triplets were clearly Up to No Good this morning.

"Are you thinking what I'm thinking?" Sassy quietly asked her siblings.

"If you are thinking that our experiment with negative space in art got interrupted last summer by our rescue of the *Mona Lisa,* then I am thinking what you are thinking," Spike told the other two.

"If you're thinking that there are plenty of objects around the house that could use some negative space in them, then I'm thinking what you're thinking," Brick whispered.

"If I'm thinking that folks won't notice the lovely negative space we have created, unless we put it in a most obvious place, such as the staircase, then I'm thinking what I'm thinking as well," Sassy said.

And with that quiet communication, which so frightens those around them, the three crept outside to the gardener's shed to retrieve the saws and hatchets necessary for the continuation of their alarming project.

At 8:00 A.M. the triplets stood gloating over the completion of their latest masterpiece.

"IT'S LOVELY!" Sassy shrieked.

"GORGEOUS!" shouted Spike.

"HOLY, EVEN!" screamed their brother Brick at the top of his lungs before collapsing in laughter at his own fabulous wit.

For their creation was holey, indeed. The spiral staircase now sported two examples of negative space. To the unartistic, it would appear that there were two steps missing.

It had taken the better part of the early morning for the triplets to complete this project.

They carefully gathered scraps of carpet and wood together and took them outside for disposal. There was a time when they might have left a giant mess for Someone Else to clean up, but not so anymore. Ever since they had almost lost Benway to Hollywood, the three had been so conscientious about cleaning up their own messes, he never even knew they existed.

No one heard the Loud Crash that followed the successful completion of the triplets' art, because Ninda was upstairs practicing her bagpipes. (She uses the bagpipes as an instrument of protest because she believes that in order to be effective, protest must be very loud.)

The only thing in the Bellweather home louder than Ninda's bagpipes is the doorbell, which is connected to a foghorn and disturbs Dr. Bellweather's concentration. When the foghorn sounds, he flings open the window of his fifth-floor laboratory and throws things down at hapless individuals whose only crime has been to ring a doorbell.

The professor refuses to disconnect the horn, despite repeated requests that he do so. One can only assume that this little game appeals to what his family refers to as his "peculiar sense of humor."

Some twenty-five minutes after the Crash That No One Heard, the doorbell rang.

Dr. Hannibal was no stranger to the Lighthouse on the Hill. With five children there were many demands for house calls. After ringing the bell, he stood with his body pressed tightly against the door in order to avoid the professor's missiles.

"Please let yourself in, the door is unlocked," came a voice from within the lighthouse.

The physician stepped inside just as a small scale crashed onto the porch behind him.

"Naturally, I would have answered the door had I been capable of doing so," said Benway, who was lying near the grandfather clock in the entryway.

After falling down the stairs he had managed to drag himself over to the telephone, which he now cradled in his arms. His leg was bent at an extremely funny angle. "Thank you very much for coming."

Dr. Hannibal settled in next to the butler and methodically unpacked his special bag, one he only ever brought to the Lighthouse on the Hill. It contained objects not necessary for house calls to any other location in Eel-Smack-by-the-Bay.

From this kit he pulled a fire extinguisher, a hammer, tongs, a snakebite kit, a hacksaw, and a blowtorch. Mundane items, such as tongue depressors and thermometers, tended to shift to the bottom of the bag.

The triplets came galloping up from the lair. They had been using wire hangers and manicure scissors to experiment with negative space (otherwise known as holes) on the Persian rug outside Spider's bedroom.

"THIS IS OUR BEST ART FORM YET!" shrieked Sassy.

"I FULLY AGREE!" screamed Brick.

"WHAT COULD POSSIBLY BE NEGATIVE ABOUT LEAVING SPACE?" yelled Spike.

The sight of Benway lying a few feet from the spiral staircase, his leg bent at an excruciating angle, answered *that* question. The three cast uneasy glances at one another.

"I'll go find Mother," Sassy whispered.

"I'll go find Ninda," Brick whispered.

"I'll go find Spider," Spike whispered.

There was no question of anyone fetching Dr. Bellweather.

Mrs. Bellweather was upstairs painting.

As usual.

Lillian Bellweather is a most remarkable painter—yet the only thing she ever paints is the Lighthouse on the Hill. This she does with abandon. And without end. Not an inch of that structure escapes the frequent touch of her brush.

One must never lean against the walls of the Bellweather home. This is something the Bellweather children learned early. Visitors to the lighthouse, however, tend to come away with swaths of paint decorating their clothing.

Sassy found her mother in the magenta room. She was painting it a lovely caution-sign yellow.

Brick found Ninda in the lighthouse library. She was reading from a book titled *Pogo Stick: The Ups and Downs of the Toy Manufacturers' Labor Union.*

Spike didn't find Spider anywhere.

By the time Mrs. Bellweather and Ninda had been

located and ushered into the entryway, Dr. Hannibal was finished with his examination and declared Benway's leg badly broken. The triplets hurried out the front door before anyone could begin questioning how the leg had come to be broken.

"Are you thinking what I'm thinking?" Sassy asked her brothers.

"If you're thinking that it is a mystery how anyone could have missed seeing the lovely negative space that we left in the staircase, then I am thinking what you're thinking," Spike whispered back.

"If you are thinking that even though it's a mystery how anyone could have missed seeing the lovely negative space that we left in the staircase, and that it's a Really Bad thing that Benway's leg is broken, then I am thinking what you are thinking," whispered Brick.

"If I am thinking that, even though it is most definitely not our fault that Benway wasn't looking where he was going, and so missed our lovely art, and was injured as a result, we should still find some way to make him feel better, then I am thinking what I am thinking, too," Sassy whispered.

The three sat on the seawall, kicking their heels against it and contemplating the terrible thing that had happened. They thought about what steps they might take to put things right, and what they could do to make Benway feel better.

Not that it was their fault.

July 8,
Cast
Removal
And
Vanquishment
Event
CRAVE minus 5 weeks, 6 days

Dear Journal,

Throughout my years with the Bellweather family, I have been nipped by potentially limb-amputating animals many, many times. I have had to eject odd hobos from my quarters many, many times. I have been made an accessory after the fact to the theft of the most famous work of art in the civilized world . . . very well—perhaps not many, many times; however, once was Enough.

Until now, I have never broken my leg.

It would be amusing—were it not so painful—that in the past I was prevented from leaving the Bellweathers by a two-hundred-year-old Oath of Fealty. And now that I am prevented from leaving only by my personal sense of responsibility for them, I have been forced to abandon this family.

The break is sufficiently bad that I have been moved to hospital. Dr. Hannibal says my leg was broken in three places. I shall have to wear a cast for six weeks and must undergo physical rehabilitation. Meaning that when I am able to get up and move around (currently I am in bed with my leg suspended above me), I must stay in a little low building next to hospital and submit to various exercises dreamed up by members of the medical profession.

I am not troubled by the prospect of running

the Bellweather home from a hospital bed. It won't be easy, but if anyone can do it, I daresay it will be I. I did, after all, graduate first in my class at the B. Knighted Academy for Butlers.

I shall instruct the family to visit with me often, and I will tell them what needs to be done. I must remember to make it clear that my interest is purely professional and not because I am lonely for them. . . .

I am the tiniest bit uneasy that this injury now prevents me from completing my task of squirrel removal. Failure to perform this duty is a Bad Thing, affecting both my conscience and the well-being of the villagers of Eel-Smack-by-the-Bay.

Still, I expect that the sanitary nature of the hospital will prove soothing, as will the time away from my duties. Even with my recently discovered appreciation for the Bellweathers, I have not taken time off for many, many years. One may even say that this break was long overdue.

• 2 •
The Troubles of Spider Bellweather and Punishment for the Triplets

Spider was among those who missed the Crash That No One Heard because he was sitting on a bench at Lymetick Park. He was not there because he enjoys fresh air and sunshine, no indeed. Spider prefers the dank and gloomy light of his basement lair. He rarely ventures from it when the sun is out, but when he must, he dons a hat to cover the curly blond hair that tends to fall in his face. He puts on aviator sunglasses to protect his used-to-the-dim-light-of-the-lair eyes, and he covers himself in Professor Bellweather's cast-off trench coat. Besides helping him to avoid the sun, he believes this getup lends him an air of mystery, which he finds entirely to his liking.

Today, heavy work gloves completed his outfit, and a tattered blue towel was slung over one shoulder.

In the bright July sunlight, boys and girls teetered on the totter, swung on the swings, and laughed and screeched on the monkey bars. The children were being carefully watched—but not by Spider.

A rather large squirrel with a distinctive black-and-red-striped coat studied them through very beady eyes. He sat on a low tree branch, whiskers quivering. When a smallish child finally wandered a little away from the others, the squirrel's focus shifted to her. Its nose twitched and it leaned forward. Spider leaned forward, too, his muscles tense.

He had an idea of what was about to happen and knew in his heart that it was all his fault.

When the child bent down to pick a daisy, exposing her vulnerable back, the beast leaped from the tree and landed on her with a thud. She shrieked and stood up straight. The animal scrambled over her shoulder and down her front before diving onto her feet.

This was just what Spider had feared. Darting forward, he grabbed the animal with his gloved hands before it had a chance to bite. He deftly wrapped the wriggling squirrel in the towel, and then secured it under one arm so that just its head stuck out.

He quickly popped a few unsalted nuts into its mouth. The beast immediately quit squirming. It shoved the treats into its pouched cheeks and then cocked its head at the boy as if to say, "Any more?" Spider complied until the animal's cheek pouches were so full it couldn't open its mouth to bite without losing the precious nuts. Spider had correctly counted on the naturally greedy nature of this species.

A frantic woman rushed up.

"My darling," she cried. "Did it bite you?" She feverishly checked her child for signs of squirrel abuse.

The little girl stopped shrieking and shook her head. Still, her mother continued to closely examine the child's skin. Finally satisfied her darling was unhurt, she turned to Spider.

"Thank you so much for saving her! I'll go call Animal Control. Careful, he might have rabies."

Wild animals, even ones as small as a squirrel, should never be approached—particularly if they seem to attack for no reason, as they may carry rabies or the bubonic plague. Spider, though, knew this one wasn't ill. He'd been watching it for a couple of days now with a growing sense of dread.

"Ma'am, he doesn't have rabies. He's an Endangered Reticulated Attack Squirrel," Spider said, holding up the swaddled animal so she could see. "You can tell by the red-and-black striping around the head, and the fact that he"—Spider looked for another way to say "attacked," because he felt these creatures to be misunderstood by society and didn't want to add to any ill feeling—"displayed such an interest in your daughter."

The mother looked from the girl to the culprit in Spider's hands. The squirrel's eyes narrowed. Most small animals look cute when their tiny cheeks bulge out with stored food. This one looked menacing. The child whimpered.

"I don't care. I'm calling Animal Control," the woman declared. "This isn't the first time a squirrel has attacked a child!"

"No need to call, ma'am. He's probably the only one around," Spider said. Though, with a sinking heart, he knew this was likely untrue.

"I'll just take this little guy with me and make sure he gets to some sort of Endangered Animal Reserve, where he won't be such a pest. Really," Spider continued, backing away, "no need to call anyone."

He waved the squirrel at her before turning and walking at a very brisk pace. He needed to get away before someone was summoned.

Thaddeus Bohack, head of the Eel-Smack-by-the-Bay Department of Animal Control was always reminding Spider that as soon as there was the slightest proof that Spider was harboring vicious beasts again he would be sent away to the St. Whiplash Academy for Rebellious Boys.

It didn't help matters that Mayor Scrunchmunnie joined Bohack in his threats after an incident involving the mayor's poodle and a band of vicious Spotted Wallabies that Spider was responsible for importing to Eel-Smack.

True, it had happened *before* the mayor started

having political problems, but Spider figured that no matter how disgraced the mayor, the threat remained.

And so the boy hurried up the street, keeping an eye out for the head of Animal Control—a gaunt man with a sharply hooked nose that forever seems to be sniffing around for trouble. Fortunately, Bohack always wears a pith helmet. This makes him easily recognizable from a distance, and Spider is usually able to avoid him.

Jogging home, Spider wished that he had resisted the urge to smuggle a dozen Endangered Reticulated Attack Squirrels into Eel-Smack-by-the-Bay.

He'd discovered the small beasts when the whole family had traveled to the Panjeeyan continent so that Dr. Bellweather could receive a prestigious award for one of his most popular inventions, the self-cleaning street.

Spider had recognized the animals from consulting his favorite Web site, www.Endangeredspecieshaving theabilitytomaimorkillinagruesomemanner.com, which featured the following article:

The Reticulated Attack Squirrel is indigenous to the continent of Panjeeya. From nose to tail it can grow to be as large as twenty inches long and weigh up to six pounds. The species is noted for its distinctive red-and-black striping and its fearless attacks on animals much larger than itself. The Reticulated Attack Squirrel lives on nuts and worms. It is believed that this last fact has led to reports of the squirrels attacking humans, as the Reticulated Attack Squirrel frequently mistakes untied shoelaces for the worms it considers a treat.

The species has been listed as endangered. Its decline is thought to be caused by loss of habitat, and the fact that it is not always wise in its choice of targets for attack. These factors have reduced the population mainly to protected wildlife preserves.

Spider had smuggled the little beasts home to Eel-Smack, intending to study them before shipping them off to the Tom Thumb Habitat for Small Endangered

Animals. Unfortunately, the squirrels had mysteriously escaped. When there were no immediate reports of vicious squirrel sightings in the area, Spider had gradually relaxed, assuming that the small terrors had somehow migrated away from Eel-Smack.

What a mistake.

Despite their endangered status, they managed to reproduce rapidly. Reports of squirrel attacks began to trickle into the Office of Animal Control. Children were usually the victims, pounced on from behind. Concerned parents' groups started calling for action. And the problem was spreading.

Spider rushed up the steps to the Lighthouse on the Hill. He needed to get Leo (for that is what he had decided to call the squirrel) inside before anyone saw him. Spider hoped that by observing Leo's habits, he'd be inspired to figure out a way to humanely rid the town of the pests.

Ninda was sitting on the top step, head in her hands, with a copy of *Hospitalization Hurts: A Guide to the Domestic Workers' Rights When Injured on the Job* at her side.

She looked up.

"Um, don't say anything to Benway about this just yet, okay?" he asked, tucking the end of the towel more firmly around the squirrel. "It's only until I can figure out a plan. I want to find a good way to present it to him so he doesn't start to think about leaving again."

Ninda's eyes welled up.

"It doesn't matter," she said in a choked voice. "Benway broke his leg really bad, and he's been taken away to the hospital. Mother is there with him now."

Spider was conscious of sympathy for Benway but he *needed* to get Leo inside.

"Oooh, that's too bad–but I'm sure he'll be okay, Ninda. Even if it's a bad break, he'll heal–and I know they'll make him comfortable in the hospital," Spider reassured her, opening the front door and stepping inside. "No need to cry for him," he called over his shoulder before closing it.

"Him! What about me! Without him to take care of, I have nothing to do for the next six weeks!" Ninda wailed.

Just inside, Ninda's voice was completely drowned

out by the sound of Professor Bellweather's shouting.

Dr. Eugene Bellweather is the very picture of a mad scientist and possessed of very *busy* eyebrows. They wiggle and jump and draw themselves together in a scowl. When he's really enraged, they shake so much that witnesses have occasionally expressed fear that they might fall right off his face.

Just now, the professor's eyebrows had worked themselves into such a state that they could have joined an Olympic gymnastics team. He was seated on the bottom step of the stairs. It was clear from the way he was rubbing his shin that he had very nearly suffered the same fate Benway had.

The triplets stood in front of him, innocent expressions on their angelic faces.

"Is it not enough that I live with interruptions day in and day out?" their father shouted at them. "Now my own children are trying to make me break my neck!" Dr. Bellweather's eyebrows leaped.

"Why, in the name of Thomas Edison, would you cut steps out of the staircase?" His eyebrows did a barrel roll.

"WE WERE MAKING ART!" the three shrieked in unison, completely unfazed by this latest example of their father's "peculiar sense of humor."

"Art?" Dr. Bellweather yelled back at them. "You call it art to cause a hardworking man to fall down a hole?" His eyebrows arched like twin dolphins.

"WE'RE SORRY BENWAY WASN'T LOOKING WHERE HE WAS GOING!" Brick screamed.

"AND MISSED ALL THAT LOVELY NEGATIVE SPACE WE CREATED!" Sassy shouted.

"AND BROKE HIS LEG!" Spike shrieked.

"I'm not talking about Benway!" Dr. Bellweather yelled. "I'm talking about *me*! A poor genius with too many mouths to feed, whose children think nothing of creating booby traps in his home and calling them art!" He rubbed his shin again.

"If this is what you consider art, then No More Art for you three!" His eyebrows stood nearly on end; it was a most menacing look. A moment later, they flattened down, making a straight line across the professor's forehead. A suitable consequence for the triplets' misbehavior had suddenly occurred to him.

What made it even more suitable was that it would keep them out of the Lighthouse on the Hill during working hours, and he would be able to concentrate on his newest invention, one that he hoped would revolutionize mining.

"You're going to science camp!" he thundered.

Spider, who had been hoping to creep past unnoticed, was shocked into betraying his presence.

"Science camp? Those three? Father, are you sure?" Visions of test tubes and explosions filled Spider's mind.

"I know what I'm doing!" the professor roared. "There's one hosted by the University of Eel-Smack! A hands-on dinosaur dig–you three will be so worn out at the end of the day that you won't have the energy to look at art, let alone 'create' it!" His eyebrows danced with glee.

They wouldn't have danced so, had they seen the expression on the triplets' faces as the three young Bellweathers turned away.

"A dig?" Sassy whispered with a huge smile.

"Sounds like more negative space to me!" Spike whispered.

"Sounds like a chance to make the world Sit Up and Take Notice," Brick whispered.

Spider was relieved it was a paleontological science camp instead of one that would allow maximum mischief. Still, the triplets' whispers made the hair on the back of his neck bristle. He shivered, then rushed down the stairs before Dr. Bellweather could get a good look at what he was holding.

The professor noticed nothing. His eyebrows were serene, and he was feeling sure that he had hit upon a perfect solution/punishment for the triplets. What trouble could they possibly cause at a science camp?

July 10,
CRAVE minus 5 weeks, 4 days

Dear Journal,

Mrs. Bellweather was the only member of the family to visit today. Not that I am complaining. The others would likely be too noisy and disruptive for hospital, anyway. Still, I cannot help but wonder what it is that has kept them so busy. . . .

As soon as she arrived, I pointed out that the sheets on my bed seemed rather more ivory than the sterile white one would expect of sheets in a good hospital. She did not seem concerned. Evidently, I am the only one who has noticed the less than perfect conditions I *must* endure.

"How is the family?" I asked not because I missed them, no indeed. I simply wished to discover if there were any actions I could take from my hospital bed in order to make the household run smoothly. (Well, as smoothly as possible in my unfortunate absence.) This is, after all, a professional concern.

"We're all fine," she told me. "Though the professor has insisted the triplets give up art for the time being." Mrs. Bellweather sighed.

I thought I detected a sort of unhappy tension in her jaw.

"Madam, do I detect a sort of unhappy tension in your jaw?" I blurted out. Really, I am not in the habit of blurting; I expect it was only the pain medication that caused my outburst. She did not seem to mind, so I went on.

"Perhaps because you have no one to run the household? I must say that I, too, am concerned," I told her.

She sighed again. "No, it isn't that. It's the triplets. I'm happy for them to discover new interests, but it would be terrible if they were to give up on their art entirely. Don't you agree?" she asked.

Journal, it is a known fact that no one ever argues with Lillian Bellweather. It would be pointless, like arguing with a field of wildflowers or a delicate mist. It is far nicer to look at her. Even her husband feels this way, and all agree that he would argue with a turnip if the mood to do so struck him.

Sometimes, it is rather difficult to be in the company of someone with whom no one ever, ever argues.

Particularly when that person is voicing the absurd opinion that it would be a shame for the triplets to give up the destructive activity they refer to as "art."

I closed my eyes.

"I should leave you to rest, dear," she said.

I am afraid I fell asleep before I had an opportunity to instruct her in the best methods of managing the household, and to tell her that she should remind the rest of the family not to do anything that would place the world in jeopardy.

3
A Benwayless Interlude

Several days after Dr. Bellweather had sentenced the triplets to science camp, his eyebrows were still serene. They swayed gently, as one might sway in a hammock on a tropical isle. "Ah, bliss," Dr. Bellweather said to his wife, putting aside the newspaper.

Mrs. Bellweather had just come from the hospital to find her husband in the aquamarine room. It wasn't his favorite place in the lighthouse to take a break from invention; he didn't like the color. Not that it was aquamarine any longer and, in fact, hadn't been that shade for quite some time. He took his breaks from work in the room because it contained the only sofa that the triplets hadn't destroyed in their artistic activities.

"I'll have weeks of not being interrupted every ten minutes by that man! It will be heaven, I tell you!"

Dr. Bellweather folded the paper with the air of a man who is satisfied with his life in every possible way. This was such a rare state for him that Mrs. Bellweather took her eyes off the pink blush walls to look at him more closely.

"Are you feeling quite well?" she asked her husband.

"Never better!" Dr. Bellweather boomed. "I'll be able to lay my hands on anything I put down in the laboratory—without *him* here to confuse me by coming in to clean and move everything! Too bad he doesn't break his leg more often!"

"Darling, you don't mean that!" Lillian said.

Dr. Bellweather looked over at his beautiful wife, a lovely woman with whom no one ever argued.

"Of course not, dear," he said. His eyebrows drooped. They never argued with Mrs. Bellweather, either.

"Benway does so much here!" Lillian said. "I truly

don't know how we'll manage without him. If nothing else, who will answer the door when you are working and I am out?"

Just then, Ninda wandered in. "It'll probably be me," she said, flopping down next to her mother. "I have nothing better to do, anyway." She was always out of sorts when she wasn't involved in a project. People to help seemed very far away and few between, just now. Lillian Bellweather turned sympathetic eyes on her daughter.

"I'm sure something will come along before you know it," she predicted, patting Ninda's arm, then looking over at her husband. "No, dear, we can't expect the children to hang about all day, answering the door."

The professor cleared his throat, and his eyebrows perked up. Could this annoyance be a call to arms?

"Surely we can just leave the door unlocked, and then after I throw thi . . . er . . . have greeted visitors from above, I can just tell them to come in!"

"Darling, it's not safe to leave doors unlocked these days!" Mrs. Bellweather picked up the newspaper and showed him the front page:

Theft on the Rise in Eel-Smack-by-the-Bay

The village of Eel-Smack-by-the-Bay has been rocked by a series of burglaries. Residents are filing police reports by the dozens. Watches, Magic 8 Balls, and colored pencils are among the items reported missing.

There have been reports of "suspicious persons" in the area and, at the direction of Mayor Scrunchmunnie, local police are questioning a group of Rhinnestaadtian nationals about the thefts. Calls to the mayor's office, seeking comment about this situation—or any other situation, for that matter—have gone unanswered. (See related story, page 2B.)

Ninda was thrilled. "Mother, may I have the paper?" Her mother handed it to her. Ninda looked over the article. "Remember the Balboas? They were from Rhinnestaadt, too. It sounds like the mayor is singling out their countrymen just because they're foreign!" Her clear blue eyes narrowed and darkened as they always did when she perceived an injustice. She jumped up. "They need help!"

She practically skipped out of the room.

"There she goes," Lillian said, smiling. "So you see, darling. We do need Benway."

"Hmph," the professor replied. This was as close to arguing with his wife as Dr. Bellweather ever got.

The young Bellweathers were of the same mind as their mother. *Something* would have to be done about household chores in Benway's absence. For instance, Lillian was an incredibly distracted shopper, and they felt they suffered greatly as a result.

On her every expedition to the market she became so carried away with the colors of the food labels that she would leave her cart in the middle of the store while she rushed to the Pinto Paint Emporium. She'd then hurry home to start a new project, completely forgetting about the food.

Despite the nearly empty larder, Dr. Bellweather

continued to insist that they were fine without Benway. Better off, even.

"He can loiter in that hospital bed all he wants!" the professor blustered. "I'm finally getting some peace around here! No more 'Dr. Bellweather, dinner is served' just as I'm on the brink of a brilliant idea! Who needs the man?"

After a few days of eating canned soup and crackers, the rest of the family had a very firm answer to that question.

"Perhaps we might hire a temporary replacement," Mrs. Bellweather suggested. She, too, was tired of the meager provisions in the pantry.

Spike, Brick, and Sassy made up an advertisement, which they themselves tacked up on the Eel-Smack community bulletin board, right next to Mayor Scrunchmunnie's poster for reelection. The advertisement read:

TEMPORARY BUTLER

Desperately Needed for

LIGHTHOUSE ON THE HILL!!!!!

WANTED:

AN INDIVIDUAL TO

answer the door, shop,

COOK MEALS FOR A FAMILY OF SEVEN,

and keep the lighthouse clean.

MUST

leave the master of the house

STRICTLY ALONE

and not break his concentration by calling him to meals.

MUST BE

quick on feet and able to avoid

BEING HIT BY FALLING OBJECTS.

Consequences of ignoring this part of the job description

ARE DIRE

and may cause bodily harm to applicant.

Interested parties please apply to the

LIGHTHOUSE ON THE HILL.

They settled in to wait for the stream of applicants who were sure to try for the position.

July 15,
CRAVE minus 4 weeks, 6 days

Dear Journal,

Ninda Bellweather came to visit me today. She was ushered in by the Positively Bothersome Junior Nurse, a girl not much older than Ninda herself, whose sole purpose in life seems to be to bring me pitcher upon pitcher of ice water. This she inevitably dribbles onto me while knocking over anything placed on my bedside table and asking nosy questions about the occupants of the Lighthouse on the Hill.

Questions such as, "Is it true that Ninda Bellweather shaved her head just to protest the low wages the beauty parlor pays its workers?"

Since the incident was true, and since I had covered it fairly thoroughly in my book, Life

Among the Savages of the Lighthouse on the Hill, I did not bother to deny it.

I am sure I do not know what the world is coming to when hospitals allow young people to bother the patients. When I complained, I was informed that hospital hosts a summertime volunteer program. The Positively Bothersome Junior Nurse is part of it and cannot be fired.

I smiled when Ninda came in. Not because I had missed her, no indeed. It was a professional smile only.

I was grateful for the opportunity to put down the newspaper I had been reading. An article on the closure of Stinging Nettle Park due to squirrel attacks was causing me some unease.

The Positively Bothersome Junior Nurse bustled around my room, rearranging things that did not need to be rearranged and eyeing Ninda. Ninda appeared to be eyeing her as well.

"Can I get you some more ice water?" the Positively Bothersome Junior Nurse asked me.

"I'll get it for you, Benway," Ninda offered before I could answer the other girl.

"That's my job," the Positively Bothersome Junior Nurse said.

Ninda gave her a hard look, and then began plumping pillows that did not need to be plumped.

"You look uneasy, Benway," she said, smoothing the blanket on my left side (as well as jostling the device which holds my leg above me). "And I don't wonder at it. It must be terrible to be here, away from the people who dedicate their lives to your comfort and well-being," she added, looking straight at the other girl.

"I'm taking really good care of him," the Positively Bothersome Junior Nurse said, coming over to smooth the blanket on my right side (and to again jostle the device which holds my leg above me). "Aren't I, Benway?"

Ninda gave my blanket another tug. The Positively Bothersome Junior Nurse tugged right back. Neither noticed the low, undignified sound that issued from my lips.

The tugging finally stopped and the Positively Bothersome Junior Nurse flounced out of my room. Ninda quit fussing and settled into the chair beside my bed.

"How is the family?" I inquired when I could speak again. I asked not because I missed them but only to get information so that I might best advise Mrs. Bellweather.

"Oh, don't worry about us, Benway. Your only job is to heal," Ninda said. "In fact, I wanted to stop by to tell you not to worry about a thing. We're hiring someone to help us out while you're getting better."

I would have sat up, had I been capable of doing so. "Hmph!" I said.

I was about to voice my opinion against hiring a temporary replacement when it struck me that while I am indisposed, it might be a Very Good idea to have someone else keep an eye on the family. I could instruct the new fellow in what to look out for and give him advice on the Bellweather family's . . . peculiarities.

"An excellent idea!" I told her. "Well, I suppose your mother shall have to bring the applicants by hospital so that I may speak to them."

Ninda patted my hand, poured me some ice water, and told me that she thought they could manage quite nicely. Indeed. We'll just see how nicely they've managed when they discover that they've hired someone with inferior training in the household service arts! Or worse yet, when they discover they've hired an escaped lunatic!

Although upon reflection it might be a rather difficult thing to tell an escaped lunatic from certain members of the family.

• 4 •
The Woe of Wodehouse Smithers

Several days went by without a single response to the advertisement that the triplets had placed.

"Do you think we should fix the wording?" Ninda asked Spider one afternoon when she'd discovered the exact contents of the triplets' notice.

"It does sound a bit . . . unwelcoming," he agreed. The two were eating a lunch of jelly on graham crackers. It was nearly all that was left in the pantry.

Spider grabbed the last graham cracker and met Ninda's glare. "Sorry, I need it for Leo," he said.

"I thought you didn't believe in feeding animals people food," Ninda said.

"As a rule, I don't–but Leo gets even crankier if I don't give him people treats at least once a day." Spider sighed and left the room, mumbling something about increasing attacks and how in the world he was going to catch all those squirrels without getting caught himself.

Ninda watched her brother go. Had she looked out the window just then, she would have seen a dapper-looking man striding up to the Lighthouse on the Hill, positively radiating confidence. From the shiny tips of his shoes to his sleekly combed hair, not one strand of which was out of place, Wodehouse Smithers was the very picture of a proper English butler. He was sure of it.

When he reached the front door, he pushed the bell with the tip of his umbrella, while maintaining the appropriate distance from the lighthouse door. At the blare of the foghorn, he stepped back even farther, then quickly hung the umbrella over the crook of his arm and arranged his stance to give whoever answered the door the most favorable impression. A glass beaker shattered to the ground in front of him. He looked up just in time to see a window on the fifth floor slam shut.

Smithers shook his head at the carelessness of some people and glanced down at the advertisement in his hand. He'd only read the first line—but it was enough. So, Tristan Benway had left, after all. Well, well, well. Smithers recalled being interviewed by him back when Benway had been planning on leaving the family permanently.

During the interview process, it had certainly sounded to Smithers as though Benway had lost control. This was something that Smithers would never allow to happen himself. Never. He had been trained to keep a firm grip on a household using up-to-date psychology, so that one's employers had no idea that they themselves were not in charge. Such techniques would not be difficult for a young man such as himself. Of course, Tristan Benway, being older, would cling to outdated methods that were obviously not as effective. Dealing with this family would be very easy for Smithers. He adjusted his tie one last time.

"BRILLIANT," shrieked a voice from inside.

"AMAZING," yelled another.

"DINOSAUR BONES, HERE WE COME!" screamed a third.

The door was thrown open, and Smithers was overrun by three of the dirtiest urchins he had ever seen.

"DID YOU BRING THE SHOVELS WE ORDERED?" shouted Brick.

"I have no–" But before Smithers could complete his sentence, the triplets swarmed him, leaving considerable dirt upon his person.

"WE NEED TO PRACTICE OUR DIGGING," shouted Sassy, opening his coat.

"Oh, d-dear, I–" sputtered Smithers.

"C'MON, WHERE ARE THEY?" yelled Spike, patting down the man's legs.

"That is, I'm not–"

"WE'RE TIRED OF PRACTICING DIGGING WITH OUR HANDS!" screamed Brick.

"I'm here about the butler position!" Smithers announced, finally managing to make himself heard.

The three stepped back and looked at him. His hair was rumpled, his tie was askew, there was dirt all over his shirtfront, and his shoelaces were untied.

"HUH!" shouted Sassy. "I THOUGHT BUTLERS WERE TIDIER!"

"I'LL GO GET MOTHER FOR YOU," yelled Brick.

"I'LL TAKE YOUR UMBRELLA FOR YOU," offered Spike. "Science experiment," he whispered to his siblings. Smithers may not have realized that Spike was whispering because he was Up to No Good, but the hair on the back of his neck did.

Ninda came down the stairs and immediately spotted the job advertisement in Smithers's hand.

"How do you do?" she asked, trying to sound dignified and grown-up. Having realized just how many Rhinnestaadtians there were for her to help, and having realized she'd have difficulty doing so alone, she wanted to make a good impression on the only applicant for the job. "You must be here about the temporary position. May I take your coat?"

Smithers looked down at his once-white shirt. It now had filthy handprints all over it.

"Er, no thank you," he said, fastening the buttons of his coat in an attempt to hide the sorry state of his shirt.

Ninda eyed him curiously. "Do you belong to a union?" she asked.

"I belong to the Associated Butlers Under Service to Eel-Smack and Environs, or ABUSE," Smithers said. "It is a professional association, but hardly a union."

"That's terrible!" Ninda exclaimed, looking nonetheless pleased. "We'll have to do something about that. Workers who don't belong to unions are in danger of becoming Downtrodden. If you get the job here, I'll do all I can to help you when you're not helping me with the Rhinnestaadtians." She turned to leave the room. "Of course, you look a little like a displaced traveler yourself. . . ."

Smithers briefly contemplated leaving right then and there. Urchins with shovels? Caring for displaced persons? But then Lillian Bellweather drifted in.

Something in her sweet demeanor seemed to have a most calming effect. If she was surprised by the untidiness of Smithers's appearance, she kept it to herself.

"It's a pleasure to meet you," she said in a silvery voice. The delicate hand she offered was as spattered with paint as the rest of her. Smithers's hand was smeared with it after they shook hands.

"Why don't we have a seat in the scarlet room, where we can have a chat?" asked Mrs. Bellweather, leading the way upstairs.

The scarlet room was actually lavender. Wet lavender.

They sat down on somewhat rickety, wooden folding chairs.

"I'm afraid the sofa in here was sacrificed by the triplets in the name of art, and we've not had a chance to replace it yet," she explained. "Chainsaws are so hard on furniture." She gave a dreamy smile. "Of course, it's wonderful when children have little schemes and hobbies to keep them occupied. Otherwise, they could get into real trouble, don't you agree?" she asked in the offhand tone of someone with whom people never, ever disagree.

Spider burst in, Leo in his hands.

"Mother, we're out of graham crackers and Leo wants more," Spider complained. A struggling Leo fixed his beady eyes on the unfamiliar person in the room. It was not a friendly look, and Smithers leaned away from the animal, making his rickety chair creak.

"Is that a . . . tame squirrel?" he asked.

"Goodness, no!" Mrs. Bellweather smiled. "Spider is always rescuing endangered animals. Why, we've had Banded Snapping Turtles, Vicious Spotted Wallabies, and even an Endangered Albino Alligator. Well, five Endangered Albino Alligators, if you count Heygirl's babies!"

Smithers looked worried.

"Di . . . Uh . . . Did the alligators ever bite someone?" he asked.

Before Mrs. Bellweather could answer, there was a loud crash, followed by a thud from somewhere down below. It sounded as though someone had dropped an anvil from a great height onto a piano. Which, indeed, someone had.

Smithers was startled. Mrs. Bellweather only paused.

Such noises were commonplace in the lighthouse. But, as was inevitable, whatever it was disturbed *someone.*

Heavy, thumping footsteps filled the stairwell.

"What is going on here? First some idiot rings the doorbell." A bellowing voice accompanied the approaching *stomp, stomp, stomp,* of footsteps. Smithers looked toward the stairs, apprehension on his face. "Now someone's crashing around down here! Is that an umbrella tied to an anvil?"

"NOT ANYMORE!" shrieked Spike.

"I GUESS GRAVITY REALLY IS A LAW!" yelled Sassy.

"THEN IT'S A GOOD THING WE DIDN'T BREAK IT! WE'D GET ARRESTED!" screamed Brick.

"When I get my hands on the idiot who disturbed my concentration, I'll pulverize him!" shouted the adult voice, the stomping getting frighteningly closer. Professor Bellweather stormed into the scarlet room, his eyebrows leaping.

Smithers gave a convulsive jerk, the chair splintered beneath him, and he collapsed, faceup, on the floor.

Leo leaped out of Spider's grasp onto Smithers's face and bit his nose. Babbling unintelligibly, the would-be butler scrambled back over the broken pieces of the chair, knocking the squirrel away, and bumping into Lillian Bellweather's lavender masterpiece. His suit jacket now matched his hand.

He struggled to his feet and raced down the staircase, nearly breaking his neck when he tripped over a missing step. It was a very disheveled figure that ran out the front door of the Lighthouse on the Hill.

Spike waved a broken stick and some black fabric behind him. "YOUR UMBRELLA DIDN'T SLOW DOWN THAT ANVIL ONE BIT!" he shouted.

July 18,

CRAVE minus 4 weeks, 3 days

Dear Journal,

I had an unfortunate adventure today. It was getting to be rather late in the afternoon, and none of the Bellweathers had come to visit me.

Not that I minded really. I had just hoped to learn how the process of selecting my temporary replacement was progressing, for a new and encouraging thought has occurred.

Perhaps if my temporary replacement isn't a criminal or a lunatic, he might even turn out to be a sympathetic sort of fellow. And if that's the case, he may be able to help me with that Other Matter that concerns me, and I'll be able to relax and enjoy the rest of this break from my duties.

After making several telephone calls to the Lighthouse on the Hill and having several Very Unsatisfactory conversations with Mrs. Bellweather, I noticed some grime on the knob of the television set, which hangs on the wall opposite my bed. I decided to wipe it off, as it is a distressing thing to discover filth in a supposedly clean environment such as a hospital room. I must say, I had always assumed hospitals to be very tidy, clean places.

Clearly this assumption was only because I had never been inside one before. Being a naturally healthy and robust individual has spared me until now.

I disengaged the device which suspends my leg above me, and then hoisted myself out of bed using my considerable upper-body strength.

Balancing on one leg, I had just reached up to wipe at the knob with my fingertips when I heard the door to my room open. I removed my hand quickly because I feared that it would appear I was attempting to turn the television to the "on" position. Nothing could be further from the truth! Television rots the mind and I, for one, would not be caught dead watching it.

I lost my balance and fell onto the floor with an excruciating thump. My eyes squeezed shut in pain.

"Golly!" exclaimed the gratingly high-pitched voice of the Positively Bothersome Junior Nurse. No doubt it was time to dribble ice water onto me. Again.

"Are you all right?" The grating voice just did not stop! "You're not to get out of bed for any reason at all, but especially not to turn on the television! I'll show you how to use the remote control."

I opened my eyes to protest this version of my actions, and that's when I saw them.

A warren of dust bunnies.

Legions of dust bunnies.

A veritable city of dust bunnies had taken up residence beneath my bed!

I called for their removal immediately. Once the offending evidence of Lax Housekeeping (or hospital-keeping) had been removed, I permitted myself to be helped back into my bed, and to have my leg suspended again. I was informed that I was overreacting.

"All that fuss for one dust bunny!" said the Positively Bothersome Junior Nurse before she handed me the remote control device for the television and left me blessedly alone.

While I realize that it is not possible for everyone to live up to the housekeeping standards of one who graduated first in his class at the B. Knighted Academy for Butlers, there is certainly no reason not to try. Why, even the button on the remote control was grimy. I rubbed it clean, and somehow the television turned on.

I was sorry it had. A local news broadcast was being televised. The top story dealt with the alarming increase in the number of squirrel attacks in Eel-Smack-by-the-Bay. According to the witness of one such attack, a young man wearing an oversize trench coat, dark sunglasses, and a hat fled the scene with the culprit tucked under his arm.

I am Quite Concerned. How will Spider manage the matter of the squirrels? The boy most certainly needs me.

An icy chill went down my spine.

This may, however, have been due to the ice water that the Positively Bothersome Junior Nurse spilled on me as she was allegedly helping me back into bed.

·5·

The Professor Needs a (Paddy) Whack

Despite the hungry rumbling of her stomach, Ninda was in good spirits as she rode her bike up to the tallest building in Eel-Smack-by-the-Bay. The opportunity to Do Good and Be Kind always had that effect on her.

The building was owned by Balfour Justice, an attorney-at-law who shared Ninda's concern regarding those downtrodden by society. The difference was, he had a tendency to represent the poor and downtrodden in court for free, while Ninda had a tendency to hold them captive in her bedroom.

The Balboa family had been her . . . guests, the year before. They now worked as window washers for Mr. Justice, and she visited them from time to time.

It was always interesting to watch the former circus performers putting their trapeze and acrobatic skills to use as they swung from scaffolding, squeegees in hand, cleaning the windows.

Ninda enjoyed sitting just inside the windows and reading to them (in a Very Loud Voice, so they could hear) inspiring tales like *Seeing Clearly: The Amazing Triumph of the Window Washer's Union over Evil Bosses and Dirty Glass.* She was never sure how closely the Balboa family listened to her, but she was grateful that they no longer tried to hide as they had the first couple of times she'd visited. Once they'd seen she wasn't planning to take them back into cust . . . invite them to visit her again, they'd relaxed.

Today she found them sitting out on the scaffold. Viktor and his wife, Anya, were leaning together. For once, Anya didn't seem to be nagging or complaining. Their son, Igor, who was just a little older than Ninda, lay on his back looking up at the sky. His younger brother Pim sat just inside the window, dangling fish in front of the nose of Elza, their trained seal, but he was doing it without his usual energy. Come to think of it, Elza seemed to be studying the fish in a rather dispirited way, as well.

Something was wrong.

"Is Mr. Justice not treating you well?" Ninda asked. She'd thought he had had an active social conscience. But maybe owning the tallest building in Eel-Smack-by-the-Bay had changed him.

"You can always come back to the Lighthouse on the Hill," she offered.

This stirred the family.

"No! No!" Viktor Balboa practically shouted, sitting up straight. "Well does Mr. Justice treat us! No! Sad we are, because my cousin cannot to stay near us."

"Oh! Is your cousin staying with that group of Rhinnestaadtians camping down on Give It Back Beach?" Ninda asked. "I just came to talk to you about them!" Her excitement offset the disappointment that Balfour Justice was a good employer, after all.

"My cousin is King of Rhinnestaadt!" Viktor said with pride.

"Wait a minute! If he's the king, why's he camping down on the beach?"

Viktor sighed. "Wars there are and revolutionings for so long, is no country left."

Anya Balboa shook her head. "Terrible."

Viktor agreed. "Topol is come here with his peoples. Always moving they are," he said. "They have no home. The peoples in Eel-Smack-by-the-Bay do not want them here. The mayor says Topol and his people steal and so go away they must."

Ninda's clear blue eyes had narrowed and darkened as they always did when she perceived an injustice.

"That's so unfair! And Scrunchmunnie! He doesn't deserve to be mayor, living in that mansion and . . . Hey!" she exclaimed, brightening. "I think I know how to help!"

Viktor and Anya sat up straight.

"That is need not!" Viktor said.

"Too many peoples there are for your bedroom! Not enough room for us was there even!" Anya accused.

"I'm sure if they're camping at the beach, they'll be comfy camping on the front lawn," Ninda said. "Just until I can work out some details and do a few things."

"White alligator will bite!" said Igor.

A small smile played at the corners of Pim's mouth. "White alligator I like," he said, giving a fish to Elza the seal. She gulped it down before turning a wary eye on Ninda.

"Really, it's no trouble!" Ninda said, as though she didn't notice the stink-eye that the animal was giving her. "I need to look up something at the library, but as soon as I can, I'll go find them and invite them to stay." She turned to leave, then called over her shoulder, "I'll be sure to tell them you sent me!"

When she got home and saw what was for dinner, she just hoped the Rhinnestaadtians would bring their own food.

Her family was gathered at the long curved table in the dining room. They were eating oatmeal. Spider was looking glumly at the bowl in front of him, no doubt thinking that Leo was going to be very, very cranky.

"I'm afraid Benway is becoming quite upset," Mrs.

Bellweather said after Ninda sat down. "He telephoned so many times today that the paint in the crimson room dried before I could get back to it.

"I finally spoke to the doctor about it, and he told me that Benway was discovered on the floor this afternoon, shouting about housekeeping."

"Well, as much as I don't like criticizing a worker, even if it's just a volunteer worker, that girl who's supposed to be taking care of Benway sure isn't very good," Ninda grumbled. "I think she spends more time bothering him than she does helping him, or whatever it is she's supposed to be doing."

Mrs. Bellweather raised a beautiful eyebrow at her daughter. "I'm sure Benway would rather have you by his side to take care of him," she assured Ninda before continuing. "Dr. Hannibal told me he's thinking about sedating Benway because he's worried the leg won't heal properly if he doesn't stay in bed."

She passed the tureen of oatmeal to the triplets, who added green beans from a tin. "He thinks Benway is afraid that we won't be properly cared for in his absence."

Dr. Bellweather looked up from his oatmeal, his eyebrows pained. "No one is caring for us now! Properly or otherwise! Benway is lazing in a cozy hospital bed, and it's just fine! We're just fine!" His eyebrows stretched.

The professor looked back down at his bowl, the rest of the rant forgotten. He sighed. "I don't miss Benway, but I am hungry." His eyebrows nodded in agreement.

Mrs. Bellweather smiled sweetly, but she seemed troubled.

"Dr. Hannibal says it's important to hire a temporary replacement so that Benway can relax without worrying about us. Imagine that!"

"Ridiculous!" exclaimed Dr. Bellweather. "That Smithers fellow caused a lot of trouble in the short time he was here!"

"HE WAS THE WORST BUTLER I EVER SAW!" Spike screamed.

"DIRTY AND SLOPPY!" Sassy shouted.

"HIS UMBRELLA WAS SO AWFUL HE DIDN'T EVEN COME BACK FOR IT!" Brick yelled.

"Poor Benway," Ninda said. "What if we just chipped in to help? I could make up a list and assign tasks. If we all help . . ."

"Well, that's that," Dr. Bellweather said. "We'll just manage for ourselves."

"THAT WON'T HELP BENWAY IF HE'S WORRIED ABOUT US NOT BEING TAKEN CARE OF!" the triplets shrieked in unison before hunching over their dinner again.

"You're right–but I have a great idea if everyone helps!" Ninda warmed to her idea. Two opportunities to Do Good and Be Kind in one day–after all, charity begins at home, and if she had to sit back and let some fake do-gooder take care of Benway the least she could do was care for her family so he could properly heal.

The triplets stared down as if their food was the most interesting thing they'd ever seen, muttering about science camp starting early the next morning.

"There's a sneaky part . . . ," Ninda coaxed.

They looked up from the green mush in their bowls. They didn't like the concept of helping, but they *loved* the concept of sneaking.

"We'll *pretend* to Benway that we've hired a temporary person! All we have to do is come up with a name! We'll tell Benway that Mr. Bunsen"–she looked at her father–"or Mr. Rembrandt"–she looked at her mother–"or Mr. Cousteau"–she looked at Spider–"or Mr. . . ."–she was at a loss as to what name would satisfy the triplets, and so stopped–". . . is taking good care of us! Benway's mind will be put at ease and he'll be better in no time!"

She smiled.

"Really, it's perfect! I'll come up with a detailed list of what needs to be done later, but for now, I'll help the triplets with the food shopping. Spider can take care of the outdoors. Mother, you can do . . . whatever, and Father can contribute by doing the vacuuming!" Ninda didn't notice the sudden leap her father's eyebrows made at this announcement. She continued, "I'll also see what I can do about keeping the villagers from rioting on the front lawn."

It is an unfortunate fact that this was a task that often needed attention.

"Tomorrow, someone will just go visit Benway and

tell him about our new butler! Maybe Father should go, since he hasn't been to see him yet."

Slam went the spoon! *Crash* went the oatmeal bowl! Dr. Bellweather's eyebrows looked as though they were getting ready to dance the Watusi.

"Contribute by vacuuming? Vaaaaacuuuuummmiii-nnngggg?" Dr. Bellweather roared, his eyebrows hugely enjoying themselves as they cartwheeled and spun.

"I will be contributing by earning a living so that this family is not tossed, destitute and starving, into the gutter! My new invention is almost ready, and now would be a terrible time for distraction! Furthermore"–his eyebrows jackknifed–"I have no intention of visiting Benway in the hospital at all! None at all!!! Who needs him? I assure you that I do not!" The professor glared at everyone except his wife before stomping out of the dining room.

They heard the door of the fifth-floor laboratory slam shut. Mrs. Bellweather laughed her bell-like laugh. "What a strange sense of humor your father has." She smiled. "Let's call our imaginary butler Ned A. Paddywhack."

July 20,
CRAVE minus 4 weeks, 1 day

Dear Journal,

It is a truth universally acknowledged that a remote control, when placed in a filthy hospital, must be in need of a cleaning. Whenever I attempt to perform this task, I manage to accidentally turn on the television, which hangs at the foot of my bed. Sometimes the grime is such that the thing becomes stuck in the "on" position for several minutes at a time.

It is unfortunate, indeed, that this is precisely what happened just before Ninda came to visit this afternoon. When I saw her standing in the doorway next to the Positively Bothersome Junior Nurse, I mentioned the filth on the remote control—and that I had just been cleaning it off.

Ninda didn't appear to care. "I brought you some library books," she said, handing them to me. Deadly

Hospital Mistakes and the People Who Make Them was on the top of the pile. "I thought you should have a look at this one." The Positively Bothersome Junior Nurse tossed her head and left the room. The titles of the other two books were Ouch! How to Tune Your Bagpipes, and A Brief History of Time in Eel-Smack-by-the-Bay: Our Village Charter and How It Came to Be.

I kept the Eel-Smack history book and handed the other two back to her.

"Are you sure you don't want all of them?" she asked. "You must be very bored here, or you wouldn't be watching television."

I'm afraid there might have been some coolness in my voice as I explained again about the filthy conditions of the hospital and the grime on the remote control.

I then steered the conversation away from the distasteful talk of television by inquiring how the family was getting along without anyone to run the household.

"Don't worry, Benway, we're all fine," Ninda

said. "In fact, I just stopped by to let you know that we've found someone to help us while you're here. His name is Paddywhack and he's starting work today!"

"He came with references, I suppose," I said.

"Oh yes, he came really well recommended—so, see? You can stop worrying about us and concentrate on getting well! Mother says Dr. Hannibal's moving you to the physical rehabilitation ward soon."

"Then she must certainly bring this fellow there, so that I may give him instruction regarding household duties," I said.

A most peculiar expression crossed her face.

"Oh no!" she said. "He'll be fine."

"I am quite certain he will be. However, there are complications to running your home," I said. "It is a lighthouse, after all."

Ninda's gaze traveled toward the door. "Really, he'll be just fine. He came with great references, and we don't want to bother you while you're getting settled into the extended recovery building next door. You should concentrate on starting your exercises."

"I believe I may—"

I had no opportunity to finish my sentence because she jumped up and scooted out the door, calling over her shoulder, "It was great to see you, Benway! Be careful in here!"

She very nearly collided with the Positively Bothersome Junior Nurse, who had evidently been standing just outside.

"Golly, she didn't stay long," the young lady observed while filling my bedside pitcher. "If I was going to visit someone I cared about, I'd stay longer than that." She bustled around plumping some pillows, spilling a bit of water and knocking some things over before leaving me again.

Ninda had not been in my room for more than three minutes. Not that I am complaining. It is a matter of supreme indifference if I have any visitors at all.

Really.

I can't help but wonder, though, why she would stop by for such a short time.

Hmph! I think the time for resting must soon be up. This family needs me, and not some wet-behind-the-ears newcomer!

Paddywhack! What an odd name. I find it extremely unlikely that anyone with such a name could have graduated first in his class.

6

Dr. Dume Is Doomed

Ninda stood before the triplets in their seventh-floor art studio, holding her bagpipe chanter—the part you blow into—and occasionally smacking it onto her other palm to emphasize her point.

"I had hoped to come with you on your first shopping expedition," she said.

Spike, Brick, and Sassy were dressed in matching khaki work shirts and shorts. The shovels had arrived, and they were off to science camp.

"I can't come with you today because I need to visit some people." Gesturing at them with the chanter,

Ninda intoned, "You three are on your own."

The triplets nudged one another, grinning. On their own was what they liked best.

She began to pace in front of them, smacking her instrument against her palm again as though it were a riding crop, and she were a war general.

"Now, you know I don't like lecturing but–"

"THEN WHY DO YOU DO IT ALL THE TIME?" shrieked Sassy.

Ninda ignored her and went on, "I need to tell you about fair trade. Whenever possible, you three should buy food that's locally grown and produced. When that's not possible, I have a list of approved food for you to look for right here." Ninda produced a list that was pages long. The triplets rolled their eyes.

"This is just in case you run across something that isn't marked," Ninda told them. "Any questions?"

The triplets shook their heads.

"Good, then I'll see you later." Ninda left, playing the chanter.

As soon as the door shut behind her, Spike picked

up the list and threw it out the window. Pages fluttered as the wind took them away.

By the time the triplets got to camp, all of the other children were seated at a table under a shade awning. A chain-link fence was set up between the table and a small area covered with digging tools and twine and stakes. Clearly, there was an un-fun side of the fence, and that was the area containing the shade awning and the other campers.

On the fun side of the fence, near the tools, stood a man who wore an outfit almost identical to those of the triplets. They nudged one another, nodding. They'd chosen well.

The man's hair was wild, his arms muscular, and his voice loud. He was shouting at a smaller, younger man who looked as though he might cry.

The triplets were quite used to their father's "peculiar sense of humor," and so they weren't timid in the least. They walked past the fence and the other children and right up to the shouting man.

"You numbskull," he hollered. "I told you this is

where we'd start, Vickers!" He pointed away from the already cleared area before turning back and poking his finger at the poor young man. "You should have known better–" The shouting man didn't get to finish his sentence because Sassy interrupted.

"WE'RE HERE TO DIG!" she shrieked.

"WHERE DO WE START?" screamed Brick.

"GOOD THING YOU WAITED TILL WE GOT HERE!" yelled Spike.

The man stared at them, his mouth open. The camp counselor came running around the chain-link fence.

"Oh, good, you're here!" said the smiling young woman, trying to lead them away. "I knew I was missing three campers!" She was actually tugging at Sassy's hand. "Why don't we leave Dr. Dume alone? I have some nice worksheets for you to color!"

The triplets exchanged looks. Coloring worksheets? This was definitely not what they had in mind.

"WE'RE HERE TO DIG!" Sassy screamed.

"WE'VE BEEN PRACTICING FOR DAYS!" shouted Spike.

"WE BROUGHT OUR OWN SHOVELS!" yelled

Brick, shoving his into Dr. Dume's face so that the paleontologist could admire the fine tool.

Dr. Dume stumbled backward, lost his footing, and fell. The smaller man and the camp counselor scrambled to help him up.

"I told you to keep the kids away from me," he snarled, dusting the seat of his cargo pants. "This science camp is the worst idea ever!"

"But, sir,"—the younger man cringed, even as he spoke—"it's funding your research."

Dr. Dume took a menacing step in the younger man's direction. "I don't care!" he shouted.

"His rant's not as impressive as Father's is," Sassy whispered.

"He lacks the eyebrows," Spike whispered.

"Still, what a sense of humor!" Brick whispered as they allowed themselves to be led toward the other campers by the young woman who introduced herself as Miss Kidwile.

The three saw immediately that they'd just spend the day coloring dinosaur worksheets and making unimaginative crafts. Not at all the sort of thing one does when hoping to get the world to Sit Up and Take Notice.

"We'll have to do something about this," Brick whispered.

In spite of the warm morning, Miss Kidwile and the other campers felt the hair on the back of their necks stand up as though an icy breeze were blowing.

July 22,
CRAVE minus 3 weeks, 6 days

Dear Journal,

I am truly at a loss to understand how it is possible for a device, which just sits on a bedside table, to be so covered with filth that it *must* be wiped off several times a day. Indeed, I believe I may have mentioned that the grime is such that it becomes stuck in the "on" position for several minutes at a time. This is unfortunate indeed.

I am not now nor have I ever been one of those slack-jawed, television-watching, sofa root vegetables (or whatever it is that they're called). The few moments of leisure I have ever been able to spare (not that there were many of those while cleaning up after Other People and Saving the World from the Bellweathers) have been much better employed in reading books or gardening. Of course gardening from a hospital bed is Rather Difficult.

But I digress.

In addition to the usual program—referred to in the guide as a "soap opera" (during which I have noticed very little, if any, singing going on), the local news station broadcasts its news at any and all hours, and one of the major stories (besides the fact that the incompetent mayor, Scrunchmunnie, is running for reelection, completely unopposed) is the growing number of squirrel attacks. I simply must meet this Paddywhack to see if he is a sympathetic sort of fellow who might help me on his days off by trapping squirrels.

My anxiety about the situation increased

when Spider stopped by for a visit today. He had evidently come from the library, for he had with him some wildlife books.

I smiled when he came in. Not because I had missed him, no indeed. It was a professional smile only.

"I am interested to hear how the family is getting along," I told him.

"We're just fine," he said. "May I turn down the volume?" he asked, indicating the television. Drat how that thing turns itself on at the most inopportune times.

"I came to tell you not to worry." His eyes had a strange look. "The new butler is working out well."

"Ah, yes," I said. "Ninda mentioned the temporary butler. What was his name again?"

"Paddywhack. Ned A. Paddywhack."

"Hmph!" I said. "That is certainly a most unusual name for a butler. Where did he go to school?"

"Uh . . . the same place you did," Spider replied.

"I have certainly never heard that name before!"

"Well . . . he's a lot younger than you are. Maybe he came after you left," Spider suggested, looking a little concerned now. Perhaps the boy thought he'd offended me by mentioning my age.

"Is he having any difficulty settling in?" I managed not to smile at the thought of his first meeting with the triplets. That would have been unprofessional, especially coming from someone who had graduated first in his class, as I believe I may have mentioned I did.

"No! He's really great," said Spider. "And he loves animals! I brought home an Endangered Reticulated Attack Squirrel named Leo. He's helping me build a habitat for him."

"I see," I said, my voice cool.

"Don't worry, it's just temporary," he said.

"I understand there are some difficulties with the squirrel population in Eel-Smack, just now," I said casually. Spider looked mortified.

"Oh, you heard about that?" Spider swallowed

as though he'd taken a drink of the ice water the Positively Bothersome Junior Nurse was always spilling on me. "It's nothing too serious," he told me.

"Hasn't Bohack threatened to take you to St. Whiplash's if there are any more problems with vicious animals in the village?" I asked.

Spider looked troubled.

"Only if he can prove I had something to do with them," he said.

"Perhaps Paddywhack might help you deal with your little problem," I suggested, as though the idea had just occurred to me.

"Maybe," said Spider. He was silent for a moment and then he squared his shoulders. "He just loves misunderstood animals."

I pride myself on being able to "read" the moods of the Bellweathers. Something in his expression told me that Spider was not convinced Paddywhack would be able to help him. Of course, the dear boy would have had more confidence in my help, I'm sure.

"Interesting," I said. "Of course, loving a misunderstood squirrel is one thing, but . . ."

"Paddywhack says he can't wait to meet Heygirl and her babies!"

I have never been to visit the Endangered Albino Alligator Reserve that Spider built in the basement of the local church, and then named in my honor. I was not unappreciative of the gesture—I had simply been so grateful Heygirl had not been around the Lighthouse on the Hill, that I'd been quite content not to visit her. It is doubtful that she misses <u>me</u> at all.

"It is not as though Heygirl misses me," I said stiffly.

Spider looked confused.

"Uh, no . . . probably not," he said. "Well, I should get going." Spider stood up to leave. "I just stopped by to tell you that everything is under control. I need to get back to finish building the habitat."

"With Paddywhack," I reminded him.

"With Paddywhack," he agreed. "He's terrific, and there's nothing for you to worry about."

"Perhaps you should leave one of those books with me," I suggested. Spider looked uncertain. "Then, if whatever assistance Paddywhack offers is lacking, I might have some ideas," I told him. Really I was hoping to figure out some means of dealing with the situation on my own. I do not wish to have to admit to Spider that it was I who let the squirrels out of the bag, as it were.

The boy looked torn, so I reached over and took one of the books from him, A History of the Dwindling Exotic Animal Population of Eel-Smack-by-the-Bay. I am hoping that it contains useful information.

"Perhaps you ought to bring Paddywhack by so that I may offer him some advice."

"No, that's not necessary," was the astounding reply. "He's working out super well! Nothing to worry about."

Hmmm . . . a younger butler with newfangled notions about "bonding" with the junior members of the household. Nothing to worry about indeed! It is clear to me, that if the Bellweathers will not bring him to see me, I must go see him, so that I may determine whether he is capable of caring for the family—and of helping with the task of getting rid of the squirrels.

I can afford to lie about no longer. Not when the Bellweather family needs me.

Visiting Heygirl, is he? Hmph!

I'll have to ask him how he enjoyed that little encounter when I leave the hospital to visit the Lighthouse on the Hill tonight!

•7•

People Helping People

Thaddeus Bohack, head of Eel-Smack-by-the-Bay Animal Control, was having a very hard time of it. He was at Village Hall, seated in Mayor Scrunchmunnie's office, being yelled at and pelted with the hard candies the mayor kept on his desk for that very purpose. True, they bounced off his pith helmet, but it was still embarrassing. Bohack much preferred yelling to being yelled at.

"Reelection is coming up!" *Plink*. A red sourball hit the helmet. "People are yelling for my head over all those thefts *and* the blasted Attack Squirrels!" *Plink*.

This one was orange. "I may be running unopposed, but it will be a political disaster if no one actually votes for me!

"Another playground had to be closed today!" *Plink.* A green candy for variety. "The squirrel attack problem is yours! Now fix it!"

Bohack flinched again. "I know Spider Bellweather is behind this, somehow," he whined. "I just need to . . ." *Plink.* Red.

By the time Bohack left the mayor's office, he still had no plan to deal with the vicious squirrel population in Eel-Smack-by-the-Bay—but he did have many multicolored dents in his pith helmet.

Ninda, seeing him on her way through town on her bike, thought it odd. Bohack didn't seem the type to decorate his clothing. She shrugged, and then swerved when a squad car (the only one in Eel-Smack-by-the-Bay) zoomed past, going in the same direction she was.

Her stomach was growling. Breakfast had been an apple and a chunk of bittersweet chocolate. She suspected her lunch would be the same.

She was pedaling down to the Rhinnestaadtian

encampment on Give It Back Beach for the second time in two days, a large book from the library in the basket on her bicycle.

The evening before she'd watched the campers from behind some tall sea grass, figuring she should observe them first before approaching. She had, she believed, a splendid plan to help, but she wanted to make sure that the former king of the Rhinnestaadtians agreed.

Last night, chickens and goats had meandered around some ten or eleven brightly colored tents. The joyful noise of small children playing a rowdy outdoor game had mingled with the sound of an unidentifiable musical instrument. The delicious smell of warm bread baking in an outdoor oven had finally forced Ninda to stop spyi . . . observing, and go home to a very meager dinner.

Riding back to the lighthouse, she'd been a tad uneasy when she reflected that for a people without a country, the Rhinnestaadtians seemed a basically cheery lot. In the light of day, Ninda knew better. They were Downtrodden and Oppressed, and she was determined to help them.

In fact, this morning's scene would prove far more comfortable than last night's. For Ninda, anyway.

By the time she got to the beach, the squad car was parked on the outskirts of the tent city. Missing were the joyful shrieks of the children. Even the livestock seemed cowed. There was a clutch of anxious-looking faces and in the middle of the crowd Ninda could see Mayor Scrunchmunnie and Sheriff Omar.

Mayor Scrunchmunnie, whom Ninda had only ever seen from afar, was addressing one of the biggest men Ninda had ever seen in her life. He was well over six feet tall and wore a scarlet shirt tied at the waist with a humongous purple sash. His size should have made him seem frightening, but despite his troubled expression, he had a kind and open face.

She rode her bike right up to them.

"Forty-eight hours, *Your Majesty*," the mayor ordered sarcastically. He shoved some official-looking papers at the big man. "Then you'll be locked up for vagrancy and theft!"

Ninda stepped off her bike and put down the kick-stand.

"Wait a minute!" she said. "Are you accusing these people of stealing? Where's your proof?"

The mayor was so startled by Ninda's outburst he just stared at her for a moment. A mumbling started among the Rhinnestaadtians. "I don't need proof!" Scrunchmunnie shouted. "These people show up and things start disappearing! They need to move along!" He turned back to the big man, shoving the papers into the man's hands. "You people need to move along!"

"Of course you need proof!" Ninda's clear blue eyes narrowed and darkened as they always did when she perceived an injustice. "People are innocent until proven guilty! You don't know that these people stole anything! You can't make them leave!"

"I can do anything I want, young lady!" Schrunchmunnie's face was red. "I'm the mayor! And you," he once again addressed the Rhinnestaadtians, "have forty-eight hours to clear out! I will not be accused of not doing anything to clean up this town." From somewhere in the crowd a child began to sob.

Ninda's blood boiled.

"You'll be sorry!" she called. Just before he got into the squad car, the mayor turned back to look at her.

"You're just a kid!" he practically spat.

Sheriff Omar leaned over and said something to the mayor. Ninda heard her name and had the satisfaction of watching the mayor's face go from purple to white.

The squad car drove off, and the delicious smell of roasting meat wafted under her nose. Rhinnestaadtians crowded around her.

"I am to thanking you," the big man said, shaking Ninda's hand. "Move on we must, but is good to know is one person does not believe lies."

"Is good you speaked up," a girl of about Ninda's age said. "Right, Uncle Topol?" she asked the huge man. Just then Ninda's stomach growled and the man smiled. "Eat we must before leaving. Join us!"

Ninda didn't have to be asked twice. She followed Uncle Topol and the girl over to an outdoor kitchen.

Near the fire pit where meat roasted on a spit, a long table was set up. There were platters of soft cheese, nutbreads, berries and apples, unfamiliar-looking pastries, and, of course, the roast.

The girl introduced herself as Katerinka, and again thanked Ninda for coming to her people's defense.

"Everywhere we go, it is like this," she said. "Peoples see us and think we steals from them, or make dirty their village because we are different."

Uncle Topol nodded in agreement but then asked, "How know you this is not true?"

"The Balboas sent me," Ninda explained.

"You must be that funny girl they told us about!" Katerinka exclaimed. "Uncle Viktor says you helped find work! Aunt Anya says–" She paused as though carefully considering her next words. "Well, my aunt Anya complains much," she concluded.

Uncle Topol nodded. "I am hear interesting story from her," he said, eyeing Ninda.

Ninda swallowed. "I'm afraid Mrs. Balboa didn't really understand," she said. "I was just doing what was best for them."

Uncle Topol smiled. "Well, do I understand that, little one. You sit with me while eat. What was best for them I want to hear."

One of the women clanged a triangle, calling the others to eat.

People came back out of tents, and up from the beach. They helped themselves to food and then scattered around to eat it. Some sat on little collapsible, three-legged stools they brought themselves; some just picnicked down on the ground. For a Downtrodden and Oppressed people, everyone seemed pretty comfortable.

Katerinka, Ninda, and Uncle Topol helped themselves to food, then settled down under a tree to eat.

"Tell me about the time my cousin family spent in your house," Topol said.

So Ninda explained to him her version of events. She glossed over the part about how the Balboas would probably still be in her bedroom if it weren't for the fire the circus performers had set. She finished up by saying, "So, you see, it really was for their own good. They needed to be shown a new way to do things."

Uncle Topol was quiet for a moment. Finally, he said, "Yes, sometimes people need to do things a way that is different. A story I will tell you."

Ninda nodded.

"Many years ago, my people were thrown out of Rhinnestaadt. It does not matter why, only that it was not right. A neighbor country, much bigger, took over. Since then, there have been revolutionings. My peoples has no country now. A new way to live we must find. When I tell the old ones this, they say to me, 'Take us back to our homeland.'" Uncle Topol sighed. "Go home, we cannot. And find a new way of living for my people I must."

"Hey," Ninda said, leaning forward. "In the old country, weren't you king of your people?"

"Is long time ago."

"Still, it was a government position, right?" Ninda asked.

"Uncle Topol was best king, our peoples say," said Katerinka, smiling at her beloved uncle. "Fair and strong and rich was our country until war."

Being a fair ruler over a prosperous country sounded like excellent qualifications to Ninda.

"Being king it matters not anymore," said Topol. "Now, finding a home for my peoples is most important."

"I know a perfect place for you to stay!" The

mayoral mansion was giant and sat on a humongous piece of land. Just perfect for the former king of the Rhinnestaadtians and his loyal subjects. All she had to do was get him elected mayor.

"And until we can get you all settled in, you can come visit me and my family! We have a big front lawn, large enough for all of you!" Ninda said, getting the warm, tingly feeling she always got from Doing Good and Being Kind.

July 24,
CRAVE minus 3 weeks, 4 days

Dear Journal,

This morning, I was rudely awakened by the Positively Bothersome Junior Nurse bringing me a toasted cheese sandwich. Hardly the sort of thing I'd eat at any time and under any circumstance. For breakfast it was Not To Be Considered.

"For breakfast this is Not To Be Considered," I told her.

"Golly," she said. "Look at the clock, it's lunchtime! They put you pretty far under after you threw that fit."

I, Tristan Benway, have never thrown a fit in my life. Yes, I became a tad upset when I had struggled my way out of bed and to the front desk in order to ask for a taxi to be called, only to be told that I could not leave hospital.

I told the charge nurse that I *knew* that this facility was far too dirty to be a hospital but that I had been completely unaware it was a prison.

This was a tactical error on my part.

Still, though matters did escalate from there, I assure you, Journal, that I did *not* throw a fit.

Before I could open my mouth to tell the Positively Bothersome Junior Nurse that she was misinformed, there was a knock at the door.

Dr. Hannibal stepped in. He approached my bed.

"Good afternoon, Benway," he said, taking my wrist to check my pulse. "I hope you're feeling better." He lowered the device, which held my leg above me, and then examined it.

"You must stay off that leg if it's going to heal properly. We'd like to move you to the physical rehabilitation facility in the next few days," he said. "It's lucky that all that hopping around yesterday didn't cause further injury." His voice was severe.

"I am sure I do not know to what you are referring," I told him.

While it is true I had been somewhat active, I most certainly did not hop around. Graduates from the B. Knighted Academy for Butlers do not "hop around." Clearly there had been a misunderstanding.

"Clearly there has been a misunderstanding," I said.

Dr. Hannibal informed me that he felt it was best that I was taking an enforced break from the Lighthouse on the Hill.

"Easy does it, Benway," he said, making notes in my chart. "No one blames you—we all know what a strain it must be for you, living in that house and caring for that family. I shouldn't tell you this"—he leaned conspiratorially closer—"but once Dr. Fizzywig read that book of yours, he went around making bets about how soon we'd see you in a straitjacket on the fourth floor."

"What is on the fourth floor?" I asked.

"Soft, cushy rooms with no windows. It is where we put people who have lost their grip on reality."

"Relax," the Positively Bothersome Junior Nurse told me after Dr. Hannibal had left the room. "Those Bellweathers are just fine without you. Is it true that the professor once threw a whole set of encyclopedias out the window?"

I ignored her. Was the family really fine without me? I am certain that the Bellweathers will have a Very Difficult time managing without my help. Perhaps Paddywhack will last another day or two, but soon enough, they'll realize that they need me—and that a substitute is . . . well, no substitute.

"Hmph" was all I said before cleaning the buttons of the remote control.

•8•
The Pitiful Professor

"AHHHHCCHHHHOOOO!" Dr. Bellweather sneezed so hard he dropped the metal spring he was holding. "AAAHHHHCCCCCHHOOOOO!" He sneezed again. He bent down to pick it up and realized that he was very lightheaded when he stood up. He felt funny.

He tried to stuff the spring into the device laid out on his worktable, but before he could get it in, he sneezed and it popped out. His latest invention was going to revolutionize the world of mining. It had a motorized coiled spring action that would allow a miner to drill and dig at a tremendous speed, and yet it was no bigger than a small umbrella. It was incredibly powerful, but so tiny and light that even a child could handle it.

It occurred to Dr. Bellweather that he might not be shaking with excitement because his invention was so close to completion. He shivered and then wiped sweat from his brow. "Ahhhhcchhhhoooo!" He put down the tube and walked over to look at himself in the mirror that hung over the laboratory sink.

His eyebrows drooped back at him, exhausted. He stuck his tongue out and examined its reflection. His eyebrows seemed a little offended at the gesture but moved very little. No doubt about it. He was sick. He left his lab and shuffled down the curved hallway to his bedroom, shouting for his wife.

By the time she heard him and responded, he was rolled up in the blankets on his bed. "I'm dying," he told her, then sneezed again.

She put a cool hand to his forehead. "You seem a tiny bit warm," she conceded. "It's probably that summer flu that's going around. I'll bring you some aspirin." She plumped the pillow under his aching head.

"I'm dying!" he insisted.

"I'll be right back," said Mrs. Bellweather.

"Will you bring me some needleweed soup?" he asked pathetically.

Mrs. Bellweather shook her head. "I'm sorry. That's Benway's specialty. I don't know how to make it," she said. "I'll bring you some of that fair-trade tea that the triplets bought, instead."

An image of Benway making soup and tirelessly bringing cooling cloths for his throbbing temples crossed Dr. Bellweather's mind. If his head didn't hurt so badly, he'd have shaken it to rid himself of the thought.

"Tell Spider to come here," Dr. Bellweather groaned. "I need him to get wire from the gardener's shed to finish my invention." He groaned again. "The patent from it will provide for you and the children when I'm gone. . . ."

Mrs. Bellweather sighed and started to leave the room.

"Lillian? Lillian?" the professor called, without opening his eyes. "What is that terrible racket I hear outside?" Benway *did* always shush people when anyone in the Lighthouse on the Hill was sick. Not that it always worked. Mrs. Bellweather looked out the window to see Ninda directing the Rhinnestaadtians to put their tents on the front lawn. "It's nothing, darling," she said, pulling the shade down.

"I'm dying," he said again, his eyebrows arranging themselves to look pathetic.

"I'm sorry you aren't feeling well," Mrs. Bellweather said, and she meant it. "But you're not dying," said the woman with whom no one ever argued. She went to get tea and to summon her oldest child.

An hour later Spider stood in the gardener's shed looking around him. Through the thin walls he could hear the voices of the littlest Rhinnestaadtian children playing some call-and-answer game while their parents and older siblings worked with Ninda to set up camp. He wondered what Father would say when he discovered what was happening on the front lawn.

Most garden sheds have an assortment of tools jumbled about—perhaps dust even covers those instruments that have not been in use for a while–say, snow shovels in the summer, or lawn mowers in the winter.

Not the Bellweathers' shed. True, a year ago the triplets had used rag-covered rocks to break the windows in the name of art, and that had made a mess, but the windows had been replaced, the glass swept up, and the shed had remained as neat as a pin ever since. Presumably Benway, who loved to garden, had seen to it.

Spider walked over to a cabinet and took a coil of wire from a space on the shelf marked WIRE. Something shiny caught his eye, and he bent down to get a closer look.

On the floor sat several small metal boxes with mesh doors that opened from the top. Spider touched one of them and it sprang shut. He put down the wire and picked up the box, examining it closely. It was obviously a trap of some sort. Benway used to complain that gophers were tearing up his lovely garden. Perhaps these were gopher traps.

Spider turned the box over, looking at it from all

angles. He smiled. Maybe he could entice the squirrels with some nuts, and after he'd caught them, he could send them off to the Tom Thumb Habitat for Small Endangered Animals. He experimentally flicked the latch with his finger before replacing the box and picking up the wire. Whistling, he left the gardener's shed feeling better than he had in weeks.

July 26,
CRAVE minus 3 weeks, 2 days

Dear Journal,

This afternoon I read the book Spider left. It had a section about the dwindling squirrel population of Eel-Smack-by-the-Bay. These animals, though not of the attacking variety (thank goodness), have some peculiar habits of their own. I checked the publication date and discovered the book had come out five years previously. The squirrel population was doing anything but dwindling now! A thought nagged at the back of my mind, but it fled when Ninda surprised me with a visit.

I was quite glad to be discovered reading, and not . . . cleaning the television remote control. Lately, that device has had the most distressing propensity to make the set turn on at around the same time every day—just when a particular program is being televised. One of those music-less operas. The Positively Bothersome Junior Nurse seems to like it, though.

Ninda brushed past the Positively Bothersome Junior Nurse.

"We'd like some privacy please," she said, shooing the other girl out. "Family only."

I smiled at her. Not because she used the word family. It was a professional smile only.

Ninda was in quite a state, I am sorry to say. Breathless, smelling of smoke, and looking as grubby as the triplets usually do. Clearly the new fellow was leaving the household to rack and ruin!

"Is that new fellow leaving you to rack and ruin?" I inquired.

Ninda looked back at me, an odd expression on her smudged face.

"No!" she said.

"Well, then has he allowed the triplets to set fire to the lighthouse?" I asked. I thought it a perfectly reasonable assumption. After all, she did smell of wood smoke. And the triplets are the most likely candidates for setting the lighthouse on fire now that the Balboa family is no longer captive in Ninda's bedroom.

"Not at all! Paddywhack is working out really well!" she insisted, looking down at her smudged hands.

"Splendid," I said, as though this were the answer I expected to hear. "You just seem a tad . . . untidy, that's all. I hope the household isn't proving to be too much for him. You know I have had years of experience running it, and of course, though I hate to mention it, I did graduate first in my class. It only makes sense that the position would be difficult for someone who has neither my experience nor my education."

I tried to make a friendly face, so that Ninda would not get the absurd notion that I was being critical. "Perhaps you should send him by so that I can give him some advice."

"Oh no!" said the poor, deluded child. "Paddywhack is working out quite well! Everything is spick-and-span, and today we had the most delicious lunch! There was meat and soft cheese and nutbread . . ."

"I do hope all that food doesn't make you ill."

"I feel great," she said. I looked at her more closely. Ninda was actually bouncing.

"You're a mess." I did not wish to be unkind, but if Ned A. Paddywhack was going to allow the Bellweather children to run about looking like ragamuffins, then he certainly wasn't doing his job!

"I should have taken a bath before coming here, I guess," Ninda said, looking lost in thought. "Maybe that's why people keep slamming their doors in my face when I try to tell them about Topol. I better go home and take a bath before I do any more campaigning."

"Campaigning for whom?" I asked.

"Topol, the former king of the Rhinnestaadtians. Remember, that group of people who've been camping all over Eel-Smack?" she asked.

"The individuals being blamed for a number of thefts?" I asked, horrified.

"Those are the ones, but it's wrong. Mayor Scrunchmunnie is blaming them just to make himself look better! Topol and his people are Downtrodden and Misunderstood by society!"

The pain in my leg was nothing compared to the one I could feel creeping into my head, for I had an inkling of what was coming.

"I got dirty helping them move all of their tents to the front yard of the Lighthouse on the Hill!"

"You didn't!" I gasped.

"There's nothing to worry about, Benway!"

Oh, my! But there certainly is! The Balboa family (who were also Rhinnestaadtian, if I am not mistaken, which has never yet been the case) had proved quite resourceful. But supposing this group was not? Heaven only knows what harm might come to the entire community at the well-meaning hands of Ninda. Would she manage to find a way to keep them captive on the front lawn?

Here I lie, and an entire group of people have fallen prey to Ninda's scheme! Unthinkable! Where was Paddywhack when all of this was going on? And how could he be allowing it? He may not have been first in his class, but he nevertheless graduated from the B. Knighted Academy for Butlers. Can he not see what messes this family is capable of getting themselves (and others) into? They need someone to take them in hand. And once again, my efforts to get a member of the family to bring that fellow to see me are in vain! He must come, or I must devise a way to see him. Drat this broken leg!

Ninda broke into my thoughts.

"It's really okay, Benway! Nothing to worry about. Paddywhack even helped the Rhinne-staadtians move to the lighthouse! He loves taking care of the Downtrodden, and he's helping me get Topol elected mayor. So, see? We're all getting along just fine without you!"

I was later informed that I was not to be allowed visitors if I required sedation every time they left.

•9•

Dr. Dume's Discovery

Early one morning, not long after the Rhinnestaadtians had taken up residence on the front lawn, the triplets bounded into the professor's bedroom. Their father was still wrapped in blankets. They looked closely at him. He didn't seem to be shivering quite as much as he had been.

"ARE YOU BETTER?" Spike screamed.

The professor's eyebrows rolled over as if trying to go back to sleep.

"SORRY!" Sassy shouted. "WE CAN'T FIND OUR COMPASS AND THOUGHT MAYBE YOU BORROWED IT!"

"WITHOUT IT, WE HAVE NO DIRECTION IN LIFE!" Brick yelled. The triplets high-fived one another. No doubt about it. They were brilliant *and* funny.

Their father's eyebrows seemed to wake up a little.

"I'm far too ill to leave this room, let alone take anyone's compass," the professor told them. "Could you bring me a cold cloth for my forehead?" he asked, his eyebrows making pitiful little motions.

"LIKE BENWAY ALWAYS DOES WHEN WE'RE SICK!" screamed Sassy.

"SURE THING!" Brick yelled.

Dr. Bellweather closed his eyes.

"I'LL DO IT! I KNOW JUST WHAT HE DOES!" Spike went into the bathroom. For a very long time.

When he came back into the room, his arms were loaded down with every bath towel he could find. All sopping wet. He deposited them on top of his father, whose eyes popped open. Water trickled down the side of the bed.

"THAT'S NOT HOW BENWAY DOES IT!"

Brick screamed at Spike over the sound of the professor's bellowing.

"REALLY?"

Sassy patted the sodden mess. "WE HAVE TO GET TO CAMP OR WE'LL BE LATE! BYE!"

Spike yelled, "SORRY, FATHER! I'LL PAY CLOSER ATTENTION TO HOW HE DOES IT NEXT TIME!"

They *meant* to tell their mother what had happened so that she could go and help. But by the time they'd packed up the rest of their gear and left the Lighthouse on the Hill, they'd forgotten.

The triplets had established a sort of pattern with Dr. Dume, which they enjoyed very much.

A typical day went like this:

Show up, escape circle time, visit Dr. Dume, get sent back to do arts and crafts with the other campers.

Escape lunchtime, offer food to Dr. Dume, get sent back to play Red Rover with the other campers.

Escape story hour, offer advice to Dr. Dume, get sent back for snack with the other campers.

His reactions bothered them not one whit; after all, they lived with Dr. Bellweather. They did notice that young Vickers seemed to avoid him—conducting busy work far from where the world-famous paleontologist labored.

The triplets suffered from no such shyness.

One morning, they saw Dr. Dume on the edge of the meadow near a rocky outcrop, far from the science camp. The meadow was an interesting one, with huge rock formations, and near them pits that had been dug and then, when nothing of note had been found, abandoned. Twine and wooden stakes littered the ground.

The triplets strolled toward the paleontologist, marveling at all of the wonderful digging the scientists had done.

"JUST LOOK AT ALL OF THE LOVELY NEGATIVE SPACE!" Brick screamed.

"AND LOOK! THE STAKES ARE REALLY HIGH!" Sassy cackled, holding one over her head, then dropping it when she convulsed with laughter at her own fabulous wit.

Her siblings shrieked with laughter, and the three continued their progress across the field. They'd found it was best to approach Dr. Dume quietly and from behind. His reactions when he turned to discover them were part of the fun.

"HOW MANY VELOCIRAPTORS WOULD IT TAKE TO EAT A STEGOSAURUS?" Spike screamed in the paleontologist's ear.

Dr. Dume had been bent over, examining the ground. He stood up quickly, hitting his head on a rock overhang.

He folded in half, clutching his head.

"You again! Go away!" he shouted at them. "I'm busy here! Can't you see how busy I am? For the last time, leave me alone!"

"DOES THIS MEAN YOU FINALLY FOUND SOMETHING?" Brick yelled.

"WHO KNEW HE'D BE SO SENSITIVE?" shrieked Spike when they'd been shooed back into circle time with the other campers. "WANT SOME TOMATOES AND WHIPPED CREAM?" Spike offered at lunchtime.

"IMAGINE NOT WANTING SUCH A DELICIOUS LUNCH!" Sassy marveled when the three were on their way back to play games on the un-fun side of the fence.

On this afternoon, before the triplets could sneak away from story time, there was a shout from across the field. It was Vickers.

Dr. Dume, Miss Kidwile, and even the other campers ran over.

Something had been Discovered.

Fast runners, the triplets had, of course, beaten everyone else there.

They found one very excited Vickers. He held a trowel in one hand and a whisk broom in the other. Dr. Dume ignored the triplets, dropped to his knees, and held out his hand for the broom. He brushed very carefully.

"Could it be?" he murmured to himself as he brushed. Everyone held their breaths. Then with mounting excitement, Dr. Dume exclaimed, "Yes! Yes! I believe it *is*! We *may* have found what we're looking for!"

"I BET IF YOU USED A BULLDOZER, YOU'D

UNCOVER IT PRETTY QUICK!" shouted Brick, causing Dr. Dume to drop the broom.

"YEAH! THIS IS TAKING TOO LONG!" yelled Spike.

"WE WANT TO DIG!" screamed Sassy.

Dr. Dume's expression changed from excited to irritated to crafty.

"Miss Kidwile," he said to the counselor who'd arrived with the other campers on the triplets' heels. "Could you please take your campers back over there so that they don't disturb anything before we can collect the data?" he asked.

Miss Kidwile nodded, dumbfounded by the discovery. She started to gather the children together.

"Oh, you can leave these three," he said. "I have a project for them."

The triplets high-fived one another—of *course* they were his favorites.

Dr. Dume stood up and told Vickers he'd be back.

"You see," he told the triplets as he walked them away from both the camp area *and* the recent discovery, "I knew all along that we'd find a fossil, precisely there.

I just allowed young Dr. Vickers to *think* he'd discovered it."

"WOW! YOU PUT ON A PRETTY GOOD ACT!" Spike screamed.

"Shhhh, I don't want to be overheard," Dr. Dume shushed. "Here's the thing. I also know for a fact that there is another fossil buried across the field, on the other side of those big rocks. It's sure to be buried very, very deeply. You three have shown incredible brat . . . I mean, brave consistency, and I know you're just right for the job I have in mind."

The triplets smiled smugly. *This* was the way they'd get the world to Sit Up and Take Notice.

"I will, of course, have to be on the other side of the dig supervising Vickers," he said. "I need you three to come here every day and dig, from the time camp starts in the morning, to the time it ends in the afternoon. You'll be so busy with your work here that you may not find the time to visit me."

"OH! WE COULDN'T ABANDON YOU! WE'LL STOP BY AT LEAST TWICE A DAY!" Brick screamed.

"Fine, fine. But you must mostly stay over here, at least

until you find something. Do you think you can do that for me?" Dr. Dume asked.

The triplets nodded vigorously.

"WAIT TILL BENWAY HEARS ABOUT THIS! WE'LL DIG LIKE TRACTORS!" shouted Sassy.

"WE'LL DIG LIKE MOLES!" yelled Brick.

"WE'LL DIG LIKE DEER TICKS AND DRILL BITS AND HIPPIES FROM THE SEVENTIES," Spike screamed, nearly collapsing in a fit of laughter at *his* own fabulous wit.

"Perfect, perfect," said Dr. Dume. "You can start right now, if you'd like."

The triplets thought this was an excellent plan. They'd been waiting and practicing and preparing for this for a long time.

Dr. Dume walked away, feeling pleased with his deception. True, he'd had to agree that the brats could visit him twice a day, but this was far better than the several visits a day he suffered now.

Much later, Dr. Dume would rue the day he'd chosen *that* spot and *that* method to distract the triplets and keep them out of his hair.

July 28,
CRAVE minus 3 weeks

Dear Journal,

The triplets paid me a visit today. Or at least they tried to. Being ten years of age, they are too young to be allowed into hospital. I must say that the chap who came up with that rule was a Smart Individual indeed. Evidently they were denied entrance, and so they stood out on the lawn, tossing pebbles at my window.

Unfortunately, I didn't hear the pebbles at first. The grimy remote control had gotten stuck in the "on" position while I was once again trying to clean it. The sound of the television must have drowned out the initial plink, plink of pebbles on the windowpane. The three then graduated to larger and larger pebbles and by the time I was aware that they were trying to get my attention, it was too late. A rock the size of a croquet ball sailed through the window, shattering the safety glass into little pieces, and landing with a thud on the floor. Through the broken window I caught a glimpse of them looking Incredibly Filthy and Somewhat Surprised. They waved at me and would have come closer. I shooed them away, mouthing, "Come back later!"

I was at a loss to explain to the Positively Bothersome Junior Nurse and the hospital maintenance worker who was summoned to replace the window, why someone would wish to throw a rock at me.

"It can't have been someone trying to get your attention. After all, you're on the first floor!" giggled the Positively Bothersome Junior Nurse.

Indeed.

She spilled the usual ice water on me, something I had mistakenly assumed would no longer happen now that I have been moved to the physical rehabilitation unit. Instead it seems to happen more often.

"I asked to be assigned to you when you

moved," she told me when I expressed surprise that she was no longer working in the main hospital. "You're funny and we like the same TV shows!"

I ignored her statement, as it would be a waste of my breath to explain again what happens when I try to clean off the remote control for the television.

I have physical therapy in the morning and in the afternoon. When I return from exercise, she treats me as though I had just run a marathon. Urging me to "rehydrate," she brings pitcher upon pitcher of ice water to spill on my bed. Then she asks nosy questions about the family and says helpful things like, "I'm sure they're just fine without you. Can we turn on the TV now?"

I shooed the triplets away because I did not wish for them to be accused of vandalizing the building. This would surely have been the case had they been caught by someone who lacked my understanding of them.

Not that such a thought would ever occur

to them. Indeed, I wonder if the family notices anything at all? A year ago, I had believed that the children and I had come to a mutual understanding of sorts. They had certainly implied that they'd come to appreciate my many efforts on their behalf. Clearly, it is expecting too much to think that a year later, they would remember such a thing. Still, their fondness for the new chap seems a bit . . . fickle. Not that my feelings are hurt. No, indeed. I am reminded, once again, that feelings should never be allowed to enter into the professional relationship between a butler and the family he serves. ~~It leads to heartache.~~ I am just somewhat surprised that their gratitude lasted such a short time.

And that Paddywhack so easily replaced me.

• 10 •

RHINNESTAADTIANS TO THE RESCUE

Dr. Bellweather sat staring at the pitiful remains of his lunch—fair-trade coffee beans and chocolate. He had finally recovered enough to resume work. Still, he was not a happy man. And his eyebrows! They were positively menacing. The professor was hungry, and there was no one around for him to take it out on. It had been a miserable day so far, and not just because he was getting over the flu and starving.

First, he realized that he was somehow missing two of the five cogwheels he needed for his invention. He had certainly left them on his lab table, but they were now nowhere to be found. Could someone have stolen them?

Then, Leo had leaped onto him and scratched the back of his neck as he had been coming down the staircase. Again. He'd shouted for Spider, but the boy had clearly left the house. The triplets were at science camp, and who knew where Ninda was? Dr. Bellweather looked over at his beautiful wife and shook his head. Lillian was a wholly unsuitable target for his tantrums. She patted his hand and stood up to clear the table of the remains of their pitiful meal. "Benway will be back before you know it," she said in her soft, sweet voice. Dr. Bellweather sighed. No one ever, ever argued with his wife, especially not him, so he did not bother to say that he didn't miss Benway.

Dr. Bellweather became dimly aware of the sound of a police siren growing closer. When he realized that it was coming up the hill, he was torn between the desire to run upstairs so that he could throw things down on the head of whoever was ringing the doorbell, and the urge to rush to the front door so that he could throw it open wide and roar at whoever waited on the other side.

In the end, the lure of the lab and items to throw won out—partly because, when he stepped out of the dining room, he noticed that Leo seemed to be lying in wait by the front door.

Dr. Bellweather stood poised by the window of his lab for a good five minutes after he heard the sirens stop. When the blare of the foghorn still hadn't sounded, he threw open the window, looked down, and noticed for the first time that an entire city of tents was set up in the front yard. He heard shouting mixed with the occasional bleating of sheep.

He raced out of the dining room and down the stairs. He was so busy wondering how it was that an entire camp had been set up without him noticing that he forgot to look to see if Leo was crouched on the staircase railing waiting to spring.

He was.

After a brief tussle, during which he managed to shut the squirrel in the grandfather clock, the professor raced to the front door. Holding the back of his neck and rubbing the scratches, he threw open the door and shouted, "What in the name of Alexander Graham Bell is going on out here?"

Sheriff Omar, the toady little mayor, a very tall man the professor had never seen before, and Ninda all turned to look at him.

"Are these your guests?" Mayor Scrunchmunnie demanded, angrily waving at the crowd spread out across the lighthouse's front lawn.

Dr. Bellweather looked at the colorful tents, around which people in interesting costumes clustered. There was a tantalizing smell in the air.

Dr. Bellweather sniffed. Was that roasted garlic? His stomach rumbled.

"Father, I meant to tell—" Dr. Bellweather held up a hand to silence Ninda.

"What is the problem?" he asked Sheriff Omar.

"These people are responsible for the theft of valuable instruments from the University of Eel-Smack," the sheriff said.

Was that freshly baked bread Dr. Bellweather smelled?

"I see," he said. "And now that you've made this

discovery, you've come on *my* property to arrest them?" he asked.

The big man started. "No, no!" he said.

"They didn't steal anything!" Ninda exclaimed. Dr. Bellweather shushed his daughter.

"This is their second warning," Omar said, looking to Scrunchmunnie for backup.

"This is their last chance. We won't arrest them if they promise to leave Eel-Smack entirely. Let 'em go to Shelbywood." The mayor looked pleased with this solution to his problem.

Dr. Bellweather's stomach gave another growl as the unmistakable smell of a fresh berry pie wafted past.

"You have no proof!" Ninda insisted.

Scrunchmunnie interrupted her. "We don't need any! Everyone knows Rhinnestaadtians steal! It's practically their trademark!"

Ninda would not stand for such injustice. "That's not fair! Father, he's stereotyping!" She looked at Topol. "Tell him he's wrong!" she implored. The big man just shrugged and shook his head.

"Used to it we are, little one," he said. "Is best we go."

If the big man left, and all of the people left with him, the delicious food Dr. Bellweather smelled would leave, too. He wasn't about to let that happen.

"Hold on," Dr. Bellweather said. He turned back to Scrunchmunnie. "You mean to tell me that you came to my home, sirens wailing, just to tell these people that they have to leave?" Dr. Bellweather's voice was rising—his eyebrows stretched. "You disturbed my thinking when I was on the verge of the most important scientific breakthrough this town has ever seen!" His eyebrows jackknifed as the professor advanced on Scrunchmunnie. Sheriff Omar had already fled toward the squad car.

"And you did all this without proof that my guests are stealing? Go!" His eyebrows shot up like fireworks. "Before I get angry!"

"We'll get proof, Bellweather!" Scrunchmunnie found his voice when he was safely beside the squad car. "And when we do, you'll be sorry!" he said before climbing in.

"No. You'll be," said Ninda softly once the car door closed. She handed her father a photocopied picture of the huge Rhinnestaadtian smiling. It said: VOTE TOPOL FOR MAYOR.

"Vote Topol," she said, grinning.

When the squad car was out of sight, the professor turned to Ninda. "What in the name of Albert Einstein is all of this?" he roared.

"All of what?" she asked innocently.

"These tents! These people! This livestock!" Dr. Bellweather's eyebrows prepared for another performance.

The big man, whose name was evidently Topol, turned to the professor. "I am sorry. Permission I thought we had."

Ninda looked around as though she hadn't noticed the camp before or the huge man standing next to them.

"Oh, you mean the Rhinnestaadtians!" she said. "Well, they've been getting a bad rap for stealing, and they've had to move around a lot." As if that explained everything.

"I told you that if you ever brought anyone to the

lighthouse, again–" Dr. Bellweather started to say, but Ninda interrupted.

"No, what you said was that if I ever brought anyone into the lighthouse, you'd pulverize them! I thought about that! See, there were too many anyway–but in any case, I'm not bringing anyone *into* the lighthouse at all! They'll just stay out here . . . and it's just until Topol gets elected!"

"Hmph!" Dr. Bellweather stomped away to investigate the camp more closely–and to see what else was cooking. Ninda and Topol followed him.

"When's lunch?" Dr. Bellweather asked, turning to face the giant man, who grabbed his hand and shook it with such strength that the professor was glad he was an inventor and not a piano player.

"So good, so good you to let us stay!" Topol said.

Dr. Bellweather allowed himself to be led to a long table that had by now been set with meat and soft cheese and flaky pastries. Even if Scrunchmunnie won the election, the Rhinnestaadtians could stay, at least until Benway was back.

Not that anyone needed Benway.

August 1,
CRAVE minus 2 weeks, 3 days

Dear Journal,

Today Lillian Bellweather managed to tear herself away from her painting project and the perfect Paddywhack long enough to pay me a visit.

I smiled to see her. Not because I had missed her, no indeed. It was a professional smile only.

I asked about my temporary replacement.

I wish I had not.

"He's just wonderful," she said. "He has such a good eye for color! In fact, he's been helping me choose colors for the stairwell." Her eyes took on that dreamy, faraway quality associated with any mention of paint.

I am sure she has never asked for my opinion on what color she ought to paint the stairwell or the kitchen or . . . or even my living quarters. Of course, this matters not one bit to me.

"Madam, it occurs to me that you have never asked my opinion regarding the colors you choose to paint the Lighthouse on the Hill. Not even when it comes to my color preference for my living quarters. Not that it matters to me, mind you," I told her.

She put her hand over her mouth. "I am so sorry, Benway!" she said. "I had no idea you cared about color." She patted my hand. "When I paint your rooms next, what color would you like?" Her eyes still had that faraway look to them. "What color are they now? It's been so long since I've—"

"You painted them a rather sickly green one month ago," I told her.

The dreamy smile didn't slip. "That's right, I painted them chartreuse," she said. "When I get back to that part of the lighthouse, what color would you like, Benway? A vermillion? Or an ultramarine blue? I know! What about a lovely scarlet?"

I could not help myself. "Perhaps you would

like to get Paddywhack's opinion." She had the good grace to look confused for a moment.

"White," I said.

"Surely, you don't really want white!" She looked horrified.

"It is not my place to have a preference, but if it were, and I did, it would be for white," I told her. No doubt she's sorry she asked my opinion now. Paddywhack would have flattered her, insisting that she choose whatever color she thought best. Thank heavens I am no Paddywhack.

I asked about the family, and Mrs. Bellweather mentioned that Spider seemed more tired than usual. I felt a twinge of guilt—after all, I was (in a very small way) partly to blame for his squirrel predicament. The twinge passed rather quickly when I considered all the ways I have helped him, and indeed, the rest of the family, over the years. All without thanks of any kind.

If Spider finds Paddywhack so very fabulous he can just ask for his help in trying to solve the wildlife problem!

"Spider seems to be spending a lot more time outdoors," Mrs. Bellweather said. "But I asked him if he was enjoying himself out there, and he just shook his head and mumbled, 'I'll never get them all.' He wouldn't tell me what 'they' were. Still"—Mrs. Bellweather smiled—"it's always a good thing when the children have little hobbies that take them outside."

I then asked about Ninda, as she had not stopped in to visit for four days. Not that I am complaining. It was just Something I Had Noticed.

"She is awfully busy these days," Mrs. Bellweather told me. "She's going door to door urging people to vote for Topol as a write-in candidate for mayor. But no matter how many times she explains that Topol held a high government position in his old country, no one seems to want to vote for him. They have this idea that he and his people are shiftless thieves." Mrs. Bellweather traced her paint-speckled finger along the color samples in her lap, then continued. "I'm afraid that this is rather an uphill battle for her."

Oh, I know all about uphill battles. Getting the Bellweather family to refrain from activities that put everyone around them in danger is an uphill battle. Getting them to sustain appreciation for the extra effort someone else has always gone to on their behalf? That is an uphill battle. Trying to keep a position with a family as fickle as the Bellweathers, while lying in a hospital bed? That is an uphill battle! Accepting that an incompetent nincompoop who can't rein in the Bellweather family (and who, indeed, seems to be aiding and abetting their chaotic schemes) has usurped one's position within the household? That is an uphill battle! Maintaining one's sense of professional dignity in the face of those who (Quite Mistakenly) believe they don't need one's services! That is the most uphill battle of all!

• 11 •
The Triplets— Thrice as Helpful

The triplets were having the time of their lives.

"MY TURN TO DIG AND YOUR TURN TO CART!" shouted Sassy from the edge of the pit her brothers were standing in. The three were being generally agreeable about taking turns—two people would dig and the other would cart the displaced dirt away in a wheelbarrow. They were impressive diggers, and the pit was at least three feet deep and twice as wide.

"IS IT TIME TO VISIT DR. DUME YET?" screamed Brick, looking up toward the sun.

"NOT FOR A LONG TIME!" yelled Spike.

Besides digging, visiting Dr. Dume was their favorite thing to do; though, true to their word, they limited themselves to two visits a day.

When the sun was right overhead, they knew it was lunchtime, and they would wend their way around the rock formations and across the site. The triplets would get to Dr. Dume's pit and offer him some of their cauliflower and vanilla sauce, or broccoli and organic peanut butter. He always turned them down.

"ISN'T THAT NICE!" Spike shouted. "HE DOESN'T WANT TO TAKE FOOD FROM US 'CAUSE HE KNOWS WE NEED TO EAT TO KEEP UP OUR STRENGTH!"

Toward the middle of the afternoon, they always dropped in on him to see how much progress he'd made and to offer their help and advice.

"IN ALL THIS TIME YOU HAVEN'T UNCOVERED MORE THAN THAT?!" Sassy would shout.

"YOU SHOULD DIG FASTER, OR WE'LL

ALL *BE* DINOSAURS BEFORE YOU GET THIS ONE OUT!" Brick would yell.

"ANY TIME YOU WANT HELP, YOU KNOW WHERE TO FIND US!" Spike would holler.

Dr. Dume had learned early on that it was useless to try and explain to the triplets the scientific reason for his careful digging. Instead, once he realized that the three would drop by twice a day, no matter what, he decided that he would continue whatever task he had been engaged in when they arrived—whether that was digging, writing notations in the excavation log, or yelling at his assistant. Certainly he would have abandoned such tasks *immediately* had he known what was about to transpire across the field from where he was taking measurements.

"ARE YOU SURE IT'S NOT LUNCHTIME YET?" screamed Brick.

"NO, IT'S—" *Clunk!* Spike's shovel hit something hard before he could finish his sentence.

"WHAT'D YA HIT?" Sassy shouted.

"I THINK," yelled Spike, poking his shovel in the earth around the edges of a hard object, sometimes hitting earth and sometimes hearing a clunk, "I THINK . . . ," he shouted again, now digging furiously. "I MAY HAVE HIT–" Dig. *Clunk, clunk.*

"A DINOSAUR BONE!" Sassy and Brick shouted when a long, ivory-colored piece was revealed.

"LET'S GO TELL DR. DUME!" At once, the three dropped their shovels and abandoned the wheelbarrow.

When they reached the famed paleontologist, all he said was, "It's not lunchtime yet."

"NO," yelled Brick, "BUT–"

"But nothing!" Dr. Dume was in a very bad mood. When he'd arrived at the excavation site that morning, he'd found a huge mess. The tent where he kept the more delicate tools had been ransacked again. Papers and pens, along with some of the finer instruments for picking grains of sand out of tiny crevices, had been strewn all over the ground–and some were missing.

He called the Eel-Smack-by-the-Bay Sheriff Association and Rifle Club to complain that he'd been burgled for the second time, was put on hold for twenty minutes, and then told he needed to come in to file a report.

His morning had been wasted, and it looked as though the afternoon would be wasted, as well.

"You three go back to your digging! Don't come back until lunch, understand?" Dr. Dume turned his back on them and continued yelling at Vickers.

The triplets weren't scared by his blustering–after all, it was no different than Dr. Bellweather's peculiar sense of humor–but they decided that waiting until lunch to tell Dr. Dume about their discovery was just fine.

"AFTER ALL," Sassy screamed, "THAT WILL GIVE US MORE TIME TO DIG! WON'T HE BE IMPRESSED WHEN HE SEES HOW MANY BONES WE CAN GET OUT OF THE DIRT IN SUCH A SHORT TIME!"

The digging, however, was rather slow, and by lunchtime they had uncovered only three more bones.

"IT'S REALLY HOT OUT HERE!" Sassy screamed.

"WE NEED TO GO FASTER!" Brick yelled.

Spike got a crafty gleam in his eye. "Are you thinking what I'm thinking?" he whispered. The hair on the necks of every living thing in the meadow stood on end.

"If you're thinking that there's way too much dirt here for us to dig bones out quickly, then I am thinking what you're thinking," whispered Sassy.

"If you're thinking that we should lend Father's new digging invention to Dr. Dume, then I am thinking what you're thinking," Brick whispered.

"If I am thinking that we should Anonymously Borrow it, so that Father doesn't find out, then I am thinking what I am thinking, too," Spike whispered.

But when they went to tell Dr. Dume about their plan, they found he'd gone into town to file a police report. The triplets waved at Miss Kidwile and the other campers, who were sitting at the table eating lunch.

The three went back to their digging. When they uncovered what seemed to be the slender bone of a wing, they were thrilled beyond measure.

"THIS IS BETTER THAN THE TIME WE MADE A SCULPTURE OUT OF FIREWORKS, AND THEN LIT IT DURING CHURCH!" Sassy screamed.

When it was time for their afternoon visit they ran up to Dr. Dume.

"A PTERODACTYL!" they shouted.

He turned around. "No! It's a stegosaurus," he corrected, mistakenly believing they were commenting on *his* find.

"And I don't have time for you today! I had to go all the way back into town, and Sheriff Omar made me wait while he finished his lunch. I'm very far behind now!!!! Go away!"

"BUT WE–" The triplets were interrupted.

"But nothing!" Dr. Dume yelled. "I don't have time for your nonsense today! This is all taking too long, and I'm going to have to go faster!" Dr. Dume realized his mistake. "But I don't need you three to help me. Go away!"

"DR. DUME–" Sassy tried, but he held up his hand.

"No! There is nothing you three can have to tell me that is so important you have to bother me now! You can either go back to your dig or go over to the other campers. But You Can't Stay Here!"

"I BET BENWAY WOULD HAVE LISTENED," Sassy screamed when they were back at their site, arranging and rearranging the pterodactyl bones to get the best effect.

"WE NEED TO GO SEE HIM!" yelled Brick.

"AND TO LET HIM KNOW HOW WELL PADDYWHACK IS PUNISHING US!" The three had crafted a fabulous story about their suffering at the hands of the new butler. They just knew Benway would feel relieved that they were being properly punished for his fall down the stairs and his broken leg.

Not that it was their fault.

They dug in silence for a few minutes.

"DR. DUME SEEMS REALLY STRESSED OUT!" Brick screamed, tossing some dirt into the wheelbarrow.

"MAYBE BECAUSE HIS FIND ISN'T AS AMAZING AS OURS IS!" Sassy shouted.

"I WANTED TO TELL HIM ALL ABOUT FATHER'S NEW INVENTION!" Spike yelled.

"Say, if you're thinking that we should do something for Dr. Dume, because he's so stressed out, then you're thinking what I'm thinking," Sassy whispered.

"If you're thinking that it would be a nice way to pay

him back for giving us a most excellent place to dig, then you're thinking what I'm thinking," Brick whispered.

"If you're thinking that a very nice thing to do for Dr. Dume would be to put this pterodactyl someplace easy for him to find, then you're thinking what I'm thinking," Spike whispered.

"If I'm thinking that the best place to put this pterodactyl where Dr. Dume could find it would be in with the bones he's about to dig up, then I'm thinking what I'm thinking, too!" Sassy whispered.

And so it was that the world's three youngest paleontologists ever set in motion the biggest hoax that the scientific community had ever seen.

August 3,
CRAVE minus 2 weeks, 1 day

Dear Journal,

The triplets paid me a surprise visit today.

Somehow they managed to sneak past the front desk and into my room. I was naturally dismayed that they'd caught me at a moment when the Positively Bothersome Junior Nurse had been called away on an errand, and the remote control had been stuck in the "on" position for quite some time. I have become somewhat absorbed in the story of John and Marsha (a lovely couple) and a Very Dastardly Villain named Dr. Knowgood. Thinking about their plight had assisted me in pushing concern for the Bellweathers and the issue of the rapidly increasing squirrel population to the back of my mind.

I am afraid I may have been shaking my fist at the screen for some time before becoming aware that there were three faces peering at me from the foot of my bed.

At first I smiled. But not because I was happy to see them. No indeed. It was a professional smile only. Then, the hair on the back of my neck stood at attention—for I realized the three were whispering.

"Hey, Benway! It's us," whispered Sassy.

"We came to visit you," whispered Brick.

"And to let you know that we've made a great discovery! But we can't tell you about it just yet," whispered Spike.

I shivered. I had always thought that the triplets' whispers were the most terrible sounds in the world. I was only half right. It was much, much worse to hear what they were whispering about. What could their great discovery be?

Oh, how I longed to be out of this snake pit of a hospital. The family must be brought to heel somehow! Paddywhack clearly is not up to the task of caring for them. Even if they are not aware of his flaws, I most certainly am.

"We want you to know that we've found a new interest," Sassy said.

"For the time being," Brick whispered.

"And we want you to know that the new butler is doing a great job at punishing us!" whispered Spike.

"Pardon?" I asked. I wasn't certain I had heard him correctly. It is not a Happy Thing to me that the triplets go about shouting all the live-long day, but at least one knows one is hearing them correctly when they do!

The three came around the foot of my bed and crept up to the side rail. Sassy put her face close to mine.

"Paddywhack is doing a great job!" she confided with rather more enthusiasm than I found necessary.

"I see," was all I could manage.

Brick elbowed his sister aside. "Oh yes! He locked us in the closet for hours today!"

"He WHAT?" I gasped, my professional bearing forgotten at hearing this shocking statement.

"And he wouldn't let us have dinner last night," Spike said, nudging Sassy.

"That's right, and he says we can't have dinner tonight, either!" she said.

"Wha—" I was about to say, "What in the world did you do to deserve this?" but didn't for two reasons: the first being that it is not the place of a butler to discipline the junior members of the household and, the second, that knowing the triplets, it was probably something I had no wish to hear about.

"What did your mother say?" I asked instead.

The three exchanged glances.

"Well, we gotta go!" Sassy said.

"Visiting hours are just about over," Brick said.

"Just stopped by to let you know what a good job Paddywhack is doing!" Spike said.

"And that you should watch the news for the next couple of days!" Sassy was positively glowing. "Boy, will you be surprised!"

Before I could stop them, they dropped to all fours and crawled out of my room.

As concerned as I was that the triplets had concocted something so huge that it was going to be broadcast on the news, I was far more worried that the new fellow was punishing them so terribly.

The more I thought about this breach of protocol, the more concerned I became. Of course, no one who had graduated first in his class from the B. Knighted Academy for Butlers (as I may have mentioned, I did) would ever step over this line. But then, neither would any of the graduates of that fine institution. B. Knighted is an academy for butlers, not for nursemaids or jailers.

Could Paddywhack be a fraud?

And if the triplets were being mistreated, I needed to let Lillian Bellweather know right away!

As concerned as I was to think of the children not being treated well, I was nevertheless aware of a small flicker of gratitude that at least three members of the family needed me. However, I quickly pushed that sentiment away as Unprofessional and Unworthy.

Something would have to be done!

No one answered the phone at the lighthouse.

•12• Dr. Bellweather's Groaning Need

"I tell you, I'm sick and tired of people coming around, telling me vote for this, or vote for that!" complained the dark-haired woman in blue coveralls. She was scowling. Ninda did her best to look sympathetic.

They were standing in the doorway of a trim house, situated not far from the downtown district of Eel-Smack-by-the-Bay. It was the eighth such doorway Ninda had visited so far this afternoon. Campaigning for Topol was proving to be even more difficult than she had feared. She had spent the early afternoon trying to convince those who didn't automatically think of Topol and his people as thieves that the former king of Rhinnestaadt had perfect qualifications to be mayor. Lately, Ninda had left him at home when she went out campaigning, because people had responded badly to the sight of the huge man in his unfamiliar clothing. She always offered a pamphlet full of statistics about the improvements Topol made in his tiny country before war had led to its collapse. School performance had improved under his rule, as had the roads, and even the economy.

Yet, here was another person uninterested in voting for him. This woman's dissatisfaction seemed to extend to Eel-Smack-by-the-Bay politics as a whole.

"What's the point in voting for anything at all?" she demanded of Ninda. "It's not like the government ever actually does *anything*! Every time someone has an idea to improve this village, it takes so long to talk about it that nothing ever gets done!" she huffed. "Well, I can get something done!"

"What's that?" Ninda asked, hoping to hear out another citizen's plan.

"This!" the woman shouted, slamming the door in the girl's face.

Ninda was so used to this by now that she didn't even flinch. Really, she thought as she turned away, it was too bad that the villagers in Eel-Smack-by-the-Bay seemed to be completely uninterested in the upcoming election.

She walked slowly up the street. If only she could dream up some way to get Eel-Smack's residents excited–something that would show them that Topol was a "take charge, do things" kind of guy. One who was completely different from the unpopular Scrunchmunnie.

Ninda turned left and walked up the street past the mayoral mansion. She needed to come up with a public project that would benefit all of Eel-Smack. A project led by Topol himself. She glanced toward the mayor's yard. Behind the wrought-iron fence the mayor's swimming pool glinted in the afternoon sun.

What would happen if she got the Rhinnestaadtians to dig a swimming pool in the public square? Or if she got the triplets to set fire to that eyesore of an abandoned building on the other side of Eel-Smack? Then, Topol and the Rhinnestaadtians could put it out and . . . she shook her head. *I'm turning into the triplets,* she thought. All she could reasonably do at this point was to find a way to rile up the voters of Eel-Smack; help them see the uselessness of Mayor Scrunchmunnie, and hope against hope that enough voters would find Topol an acceptable alternative. What would Benway advise?

Ninda turned the corner and was surprised to see Spider. "Are you okay?" she asked, taking in his appearance. The hem of his trench coat was stained as though he had been kneeling in the mud, and his hands were filthy, as if he had been digging with them. Really, he looked as grubby as the triplets usually did.

Benway needed to come back, and soon.

Spider was holding a triangular doorstop and a tennis ball. He looked worried.

"Are you okay?" she asked again.

Spider heaved a sigh. "I think I'm in trouble," he admitted. He explained that he'd been digging holes and setting traps for the Endangered Reticulated Attack Squirrels but that he hadn't caught any so far.

"Someone is playing tricks on me." He frowned. "It can't be Bohack, because he would have hauled me off to St. Whiplash's by now. Whoever is doing this is letting the squirrels out of the traps but putting weird things like this in." He held up the wedge and the ball.

"I wonder why," Ninda said.

"Who knows?" Spider replied as they walked toward the Lighthouse on the Hill together. "I'm tempted to go ask Benway what he thinks. I can't wait for him to come home."

Ninda nodded.

When the pair entered the house, they were greeted by the sound of groaning coming from upstairs. They rushed upstairs to find their mother coming out of her bedroom.

"Is there something wrong with Father?" Ninda asked.

"Is he sick again?"

Lillian Bellweather shook her head. There was silver paint in her hair. "I'm afraid your father is suffering from indigestion," she said. "I told him that too much of that spicy Rhinnestaadtian food would hurt his stomach. . . ."

Inside the bedroom, Eugene Bellweather groaned louder. Once again, he was dying. He was sure of it. He chewed on the peppermint his wife left with him. It was Benway's cure for indigestion, although she didn't grind it up and put it into warm water the way Benway always did. The professor groaned again, his eyebrows curling into themselves.

When *was* the man coming back?

Not that anyone needed Benway, he thought.

His eyebrows disagreed.

He groaned again.

His stomach disagreed, too.

August 4,
CRAVE minus 2 weeks

Dear Journal,

During my hospital stay, which has been full of Strange and Unsatisfying visits (indeed, knowing the Bellweather family, how could one have expected any less?), today's visit from Mrs. Bellweather was perhaps the Strangest and Most Unsatisfying of all.

I had been so anxious for her to arrive that I could barely pay attention to the fact that John and Marsha were to be married. I hoped that Dr. Knowgood would leave them alone, but I had a suspicion that he would not.

Just as my thumb was about to test the grime again, Mrs. Bellweather floated in, bearing tales of the oh-so-brilliant Paddywhack.

"I have something important to discuss with you," I told her before she could say another word. "I do not wish to criticize my temporary replacement. Indeed, I believe it would be Most Unprofessional to do so. However, I believe that this Paddywhack has not been treating the triplets properly."

Mrs. Bellweather looked utterly unconcerned. "Bridle-wreath yellow is so pale a yellow that it looks almost white," she said. "Wouldn't you perhaps like that for your rooms?"

"White," I said firmly. "Mrs. Bellweather, did you not hear me? I believe that this Paddywhack fellow is not treating the triplets properly! I do not wish to criticize anything that has happened in my absence, but I am Quite Concerned."

She leaned over and patted my hand. "I'm sure it's fine," she said.

"They have been locked in a closet and denied meals, Mrs. Bellweather! I do not think it's fine!" I am afraid my voice was growing rather loud.

She cocked her head at me. "How did you hear of this, dear?" she asked.

"The triplets told me when they stopped in to visit. "They are mischievous, I'll admit. And sometimes they have been known to . . . omit certain things. But I have never known those three to lie!"

"No . . . ," said Mrs. Bellweather. "They don't tend to." The words came out hesitantly, as though she were considering the idea that the triplets might, in fact, have been untruthful with me.

"Surely, they are being truthful," I pressed.

"Well, you mustn't worry too much over them. They'll be fine," said Mrs. Bellweather finally.

And then, Journal, the woman who has never believed in discipline for her children ("I don't believe in crushing the little dears' spirits"), calmly stood, preparing to leave although she had just arrived. Of course, I shouldn't have been surprised. She was probably in a hurry to get back to the Lighthouse on the Hill so that she could have that fraud

Paddywhack help her choose the colors for my quarters!

She wiggled her fingers in a small good-bye gesture and then left!

I am afraid that I cannot wait until I have been discharged to return to the Lighthouse on the Hill. I have had my doubts about Paddywhack's fitness for the position, but now I know I must return in order to protect the triplets.

As a general rule, I believe that they can take quite good care of themselves, but their meek acceptance of their punishment was a new development, and one I did not like at all.

Yes, something would have to be done. I could remain away from the Lighthouse on the Hill no more. Broken limbs and physical therapy notwithstanding.

Having not met with success the last time I tried to leave hospital by conventional means (i.e., the front door), I resolved to exit through the window.

This was a mistake.

One that was explained to me as I was bundled into a straitjacket and hauled off to the fourth floor of the hospital.

13 (Post) Midnight Adventure

The triplets left the Lighthouse on the Hill in the middle of the night. They'd had to wait a long time because it seemed that Rhinnestaadtians liked the nighttime and stayed up later than anyone else they knew.

Spike, Brick, and Sassy would have greatly enjoyed the festive air of the front yard of the Lighthouse on the Hill—complete with lively music from unfamiliar-sounding instruments—if they hadn't been trying to slip out of the house to perform a task in anonymity.

Nighttime, the three had learned over the years,

was the best time for performing tasks that required one to be anonymous.

Finally, when things quieted down enough that the three could sneak out, they carried Dr. Bellweather's latest invention with them. They needed to dig quickly, and this new device was ideally suited to the task. It was an unfortunate thing that Dr. Bellweather was not feeling better, but it made Anonymously Borrowing the digging machine that much easier.

Wearing black windbreakers (which they considered to be fashionably secretive *and* cozy), woolen beanies, and black jeans, they'd just hopped a low stone wall at the bottom of the hill (stopping to admire the VOTE TOPOL poster Ninda had plastered there), when they were startled by a voice asking, "Just what are you three doing?" The question was accompanied by a blindingly powerful flashlight pointed in their direction.

The triplets froze. After a heart-stopping moment, Sassy whispered, "Spider!"

"We're helping Dr. Dume!" Brick whispered.

"We're pretty sure he'll dig his surprise!" Spike

laughed so hard, he nearly choked. Sassy and Brick had to pound him on the back to get him to stop.

"What are *you* doing?" they asked when Spike had recovered, and Spider had turned the flashlight aside so that they could see him holding a little mesh box in his other hand.

Spider sighed. "Fighting a losing battle."

The triplets leaned against the shelter of the low wall while Spider told them about the Endangered Reticulated Attack Squirrel problem and his part in it.

They were suitably impressed.

"So it's your fault that parks are being closed?" Sassy whispered.

"You know a park with no children in it is kind of like a painting with negative space!" Spike whispered.

"And what could be negative about that?" Brick whispered.

"Oh, I don't know . . . the fact that Thaddeus Bohack could put me away for so long you three will be tripping over your beards before I'm released," Spider said. "Except for you, Sassy," he said when she looked offended.

"So what are you going to do?" Sassy asked, to show the offense had been forgiven.

"Say, maybe you can help me!" Spider perked up, looking hopeful. "My plan requires a lot of sneaking around at night."

The triplets nudged one another and grinned. Sneaking around at night was what they did best. Besides creating art and excavating dinosaur bones, of course.

"I need someone to help set and watch the traps I've been putting out," Spider explained, pointing at the mesh box. "I was going to catch as many of the squirrels as I could and send them to the Tom Thumb Reserve for Small Endangered Animals, but someone is messing with the traps!"

"Who?" Sassy whispered.

"What?" Brick whispered.

"How?" Spike whispered.

Spider shivered, and the hair on the back of his neck stood up.

"I don't know who. Only, it can't be Bohack, because if he knew for sure about this, he'd have already hauled me off. All I know is that I bury these traps—the Reticulated Attack Squirrel is a burrowing animal, you know—and when I go to check them, there are never animals in the boxes."

"Maybe they're too smart to get caught?" Sassy said.

"Maybe," Spider agreed. "They are smart, but what's weird is that someone keeps putting stuff inside." He held up the trap and through the mesh, the triplets could see colored pencils and a Magic 8 Ball.

"Cool," Brick said.

"If we catch the person who's doing this, do we get to keep the stuff?" Sassy wanted to know.

"I'll think about it," Spider said.

"We'll start tomorrow." Spike nudged the others. They already had a project for this night.

Spider sighed. He would have liked help right away but, in the end, the promise of help was better than none at all.

The triplets said good-bye and left, weaving in and out of shadows, down the hill, and through the slumbering village of Eel-Smack-by-the-Bay.

When they got to the dig site they took several

trips across the field, carrying pterodactyl bones, some of which were quite heavy. Then they had to dig up the rest of Dr. Dume's stegosaurus. This was easily accomplished with Dr. Bellweather's handy new tool. It spun and buzzed and whirled and dug magnificently.

The triplets were in awe, but by the time the stegosaurus fossils had been dug up, they felt they'd certainly earned a break. They settled around the pit they'd dug to enjoy a snack before they buried everything together.

"NOTHING BEETS APPLESAUCE!" Brick told his siblings.

They rolled around shrieking with laughter and scattering their thermoses which were, of course, filled with their new favorite snack–applesauce and beets. Finally, they managed to get themselves under control and back to work–combining and reburying all of the fossils, then expertly tamping down the dirt. It looked only slightly disturbed–certainly no more than it had been when Dr. Dume was so carefully uncovering his find. Of this they were sure.

Feeling smug, they made their way back toward the Lighthouse on the Hill.

"We'll be famous, even if no one knows it!" Spike whispered.

"Dr. Dume is going to be so happy!" Sassy whispered.

"Are you sure he won't be dino-sore?" whispered Brick, laughing like a very quiet hyena and opening the front door.

Leo the squirrel scrambled to get out. Sassy was too quick for him. She grasped him firmly, then took him downstairs and shut him in the lair. Spider had impressed upon her (and all of his siblings) that creatures such as Attack Squirrels could possibly be injured out in the world where they were misunderstood by the rest of society.

It was very late at night—or very early in the morning—when the three were cozily tucked into bed.

"Maybe, once science camp is done, we can start an art project with found objects!" Spike whispered.

"Life just gets better and better!" Sassy whispered.

"For us, anyway," Brick whispered.

August 5,
CRAVE minus 1 week, 6 days

Dear Journal,

The soft room on the fourth floor is quite poorly constructed. The door has no handle on the inside. It was quite vexing to discover this when I had awakened from a nap that I had not expected to take.

I am sure I do not know how I managed to fall asleep so quickly, given my agitated state last night! I had been halfway out the window, still wearing my pajamas (I had decided that there was no time to waste, and so had not properly dressed), when I heard a squeal from the Positively Bothersome Junior Nurse. She called for help before I managed to escape. I felt strong arm's grasp my legs, pulling me back in through the window, and then the prick of a needle.

I took a nap.

I woke up in the soft room.

None of the Bellweathers came to visit me there.

Dr. Hannibal came in at one point, shook his head, and said, "Dr. Fizzywig won the bet."

After what seemed like hours of quiet conversation, I was returned to my old room, where Mrs. Bellweather was waiting for me.

I did not wish to visit the fourth floor again, but I was anxious on behalf of the triplets. I needed to make her see that they were not being treated well. She spoke before I could.

"Dear, I'm told you were very upset yesterday and that it was because you felt Paddywhack was treating the children harshly."

"I would certainly call locking children in a closet for hours treating them harshly, madam," I told her.

Mrs. Bellweather reached over and touched me softly on the shoulder. "I can promise you, Benway, that Paddywhack is not mistreating them."

"You believe they are not being truthful with me?" I asked. "I have never known them to out-and-out lie," I argued. She looked troubled.

"I can promise you that the triplets are in no danger from Paddywhack," she said finally, in the tone of one with whom others never, ever argue.

Before I could be the first to do so, she held up her hand. "If you like, I will have them telephone you later to reassure you themselves."

I almost wish they hadn't.

They telephoned less than an hour after their mother left my bedside. The call came at a Most Inopportune Time.

"WE JUST WANT TO TELL YOU THAT WE'RE FINE!" they screamed into my ear.

I asked, "Why in the world did you tell me that you were being punished by Paddywhack?" I then quickly moved the phone away from my ear.

"WE KNEW YOU'D FEEL BETTER IF WE WERE BEING PUNISHED FOR BREAKING YOUR LEG!" they shouted in unison. They stayed on the phone for several more minutes, assuring me that they were fine. Though they spoke, as usual, at an Extremely Loud Decibel, I barely heard them.

What did that say about their opinion of me, that they should think that I wished for them to be punished so terribly? Did they truly believe I was so monstrous that I would be happy if they suffered? Then, another nasty thought intruded.

This must mean that they, too, were fans of Paddywhack. As much as it disturbed me to think that most of the family had fallen under his spell, I had hoped that at least the triplets still preferred me. Clearly, the whole family was Quite Attached to the scoundrel. The fact that the children actually lied to me told me their regard for me was weak. For all of their shenanigans, I had come to believe that their characters were sound, and it grieved me to think that they were not. Of course, Paddywhack, being a fraud himself, would not worry over this, as I did. It made me wonder if the Lighthouse on the Hill was no longer the place for me. Indeed, it was impossible for me to enjoy the wedding of John and Marsha. I was, however, glad to see that Dr. Knowgood did not enjoy it, either.

14
Spider in Peril

Two days after Benway's "visit to the fourth floor," Thaddeus Bohack stood first on one foot, then the other, waiting for Mayor Scrunchmunnie to finish his meeting with the Eel-Smack-by-the-Bay Village Council.

True, he could have met with the mayor earlier, but even in his excited state, he preferred to wait until the mayor's supply of hard candy had been depleted. Just in case.

The mayor had a very bad temper these days. Squirrel attacks were becoming more frequent. Children under the age of eight had to be escorted everywhere; they couldn't even take out the trash by themselves. Burglaries were becoming more regular, too. Every day there were new reports of scissors and dollhouse furniture and soap dishes being stolen. Villagers in Eel-Smack-by-the-Bay had had it with their town's government and its lack of action. They were tired of being terrorized by squirrels and theft. Citizens marched around in front of Village Hall, carrying signs that said things like SCRUNCHMUNNIE'S A RAT IF HE DOESN'T GET RID OF THE SQUIRRELS. True, this effort had been started by Ninda and the Rhinnestaadtians, but they had quickly been joined by others.

Bohack hoped the mayor's mood would improve once he saw what he had discovered. When the council members had filed out, grumbling and dotted with small bits of color, he slipped into the mayor's office with a very slim volume and a very fat atlas tucked under his arm.

"What is it?" the mayor demanded.

Bohack was almost dancing.

"I've got him!" His raspy voice was gleeful. "I've

finally got the little so-and-so! These squirrel attacks are all Spider Bellweather's fault—and I have proof!"

He opened the large atlas and pointed to a continent halfway around the world from the one that was home to Eel-Smack-by-the-Bay. "I always knew there was something unnatural about them, so I looked for a picture and found out that the critters we're seeing around town aren't from here! They're Endangered Reticulated Attack Squirrels, and they belong on this continent," he explained, pointing to the map.

In the temporary silence of the mayor's office, the protesters could be heard chanting in front of Village Hall. Scrunchmunnie looked at Bohack. "And this proves Spider Bellweather is responsible because . . . ?" the mayor asked quietly.

"Squirrels don't swim!" Bohack exclaimed, then, realizing the mayor needed more explanation, he went on. "The whole crazy family went over there when the professor won an award. Look!" Bohack opened the (extremely) slim volume titled *Residents of Eel-Smack-by-the-Bay Who Have Won Important Awards*, and pointed to a photograph of Dr. Bellweather accepting his award in Klativostock, which is on the continent of Panjeeya. The professor's expression was unreadable, but his eyebrows seemed to be bowing. The rest of the family stood in the background. Bohack took out a magnifying glass and offered it to the mayor. "See?" he asked.

The mayor moved the magnifying glass over the slightly grainy picture–slowing it when he got to Spider. A tiny head peeked out of the sport coat the boy was wearing. And another peeked out from underneath his jaunty cap. One could tell by the distinctive markings on those heads that they were most definitely Endangered Reticulated Attack Squirrels.

Bohack cackled. "It's St. Whiplash's for the boy, now!"

Scrunchmunnie put down the magnifying glass.

"And this solves the pressing problem of the squirrel attacks, how?" he asked. The mayor's voice had an edge to it that made Bohack uncomfortable.

"Well, now . . . you see . . . the village will be safe from other dangerous beasts in the future . . . because,

because . . . I finally get to haul Spider off. . . ." The dogcatcher's voice was uncertain.

"The future?" the mayor repeated. "I'll tell you about the future, Bohack! The election is the day after tomorrow! Two weeks ago, I was running unopposed!" The mayor stood. "Now, thanks to you and the fact that you can't take care of this varmint problem, there's some write-in candidate I've never heard of! And do you know what?" Scrunchmunnie's voice got louder. "If he wins, I have no place to live! And that means I. Will. Be. Coming. To. Live. With. YOU!" He picked up the candy dish and Bohack ran.

The noise of the protesters drowned out the sound of the candy dish crashing against the wall.

Ninda was, of course, in the thick of it all–playing her bagpipes, shouting slogans, passing out flyers, and generally stirring things up when they looked to be in danger of dying down.

Had the mayor bothered to go outside to view the protest more closely, he would have been even more furious. The flyers Ninda was passing out were urging the residents of Eel-Smack to vote for Topol for mayor.

On the flyer was a black-and-white photograph of the giant man kissing a baby. Underneath it said: VOTE TOPOL—HE'LL STEAL YOUR HEART BUT NOTHING ELSE.

August 6,
CRAVE minus 1 week, 5 days

Dear Journal,

Today began as an exceedingly boring day. My only visitor was the Extremely Bothersome Junior Nurse, who came in to spill ice water on me and to ask more of her nosy questions.

None of the Bellweathers came to see me. Not that I had expected them to, after all. How could I hope to compete with that viper Paddywhack? The whole family obviously prefers him.

Then a new and altogether awful thought occurred to me.

Suppose the Bellweathers did not want me back?

It is one thing to contemplate retirement to a

place Far, Far Away, when it is one's own idea. It is an entirely different thing to be forced to do so.

Suppose they are blissfully happy with Paddywhack and intend to keep him on, not caring that he possesses neither my education nor my professionalism. Could the Bellweather family really be so taken with such a man?

Of course, they are free to hire whomever they wish. However, Paddywhack's inability to take the family in hand, and his newfangled notions about "bonding" with Spider and Ninda, make it seem unlikely that he graduated from the same establishment I did. This is merely a Professional Observation, and not a personal one.

The B. Knighted Academy for Butlers is an Old and Fine institution, and I am sorry to say that it is not unheard of for deceitful domestic servants to claim they have attended school there, when they have not. These imposters believe, and rightly so, that the very name lends prestige. Presenting false information is a despicable practice.

Surely, if this were the case for Paddywhack, the Bellweathers would have to let him go. No matter how "attached" they fancied themselves to be.

My heart thumped a bit as I reached for the telephone and dialed the old number. There was no answer. I left a message for Phileas Pogonip, keeper of Academy records, requesting that he telephone me back right away, as there was an urgent matter I wished to discuss.

While I waited for him to return my call, I read one of the books Ninda had brought me, A Brief History of Time in Eel-Smack-by-the-Bay. As fascinating as the tome was, I only managed to read thirty pages or so before turning my attention to the cleaning of the remote control device.

In spite of my anxiety regarding the possible imposter Paddywhack, I soon became absorbed in an educational program about wild creatures, great and small.

One animal featured was a species of squirrel

that had once lived in a part of the world where there was famine, and so learned to steal whatever it could. The presentation was mesmerizing, but it caused me to reach for the wildlife book I'd borrowed from Spider.

I had just turned to the page about squirrels native to Eel-Smack-by-the-Bay, when a news broadcaster interrupted (without excusing himself, mind you) the nature program with a special bulletin.

He was standing in a rocky field on the outskirts of Eel-Smack, babbling about an amazing new find. He introduced Dr. Dume of the University of Eel-Smack-by-the-Bay.

Dr. Dume is a tweedy-looking fellow with unkempt hair and large arms—the filthiness of which put me in mind of the triplets. Nevertheless, he speaks with great authority.

"I made this truly remarkable find this afternoon at approximately one fifteen P.M. What we have here is an entirely unknown species of dinosaur!" he said. "The fossils are similar to those of the stegosaurus, though I knew very early on that I had something much more significant here—and I was right! I also discovered the fossilized remains of wings. This beast must have weighed close to three thousand pounds, and yet most assuredly took to the sky, in what must have been a spectacular way. Truly the important find of the century, and I made it! I have already telephoned my fellow scientists the world over to tell them of my amazing discovery—many are on their way from distant parts of the globe to see the remarkable fossil I have named the Dumeasaur."

Well, that fellow was certainly proud of himself! The subject only vaguely interested me and I was just about to switch to a different channel when I caught sight of a child with curly golden hair standing in the crowd. I choked on my ice water and blinked. There were three of them. I felt faint at the thought of what they could possibly be up to and decided I did not want to know.

I changed the channel. The content of the new channel certainly was not my fault.

John and Marsha were happily married, after all—a surprising thing, since John and Dr. Knowgood turned out to be identical twins separated at birth. Not that I had any interest that nonsense.

• 15 •
Charmed, I'm Sure

Ninda was sure that she had hit upon the campaign slogan to beat all campaign slogans, but later that afternoon, when she showed the poster to Spider, he was dubious.

"Do you think it's a good idea to bring up the whole stealing thing?" he asked.

They were sitting on the floor in the front hall of the Lighthouse on the Hill. It was not the most comfortable place in the house, but a new and alarming development had occurred. One that required Spider to guard the front door.

Leo the squirrel was nuts. (And this is saying something, considering the naturally crazed state of Endangered Reticulated Attack Squirrels.)

Up until very recently, Leo had seemed quite content to stay inside, attacking Dr. Bellweather when he felt like it and accepting treats from Spider. In the past few days, this had changed dramatically. He was frenzied, trying constantly to escape the Lighthouse on the Hill.

He haunted the vestibule, and anytime someone opened the front door, he would try to dart through. This, coupled with concern about the mysterious stranger who taunted Spider daily by leaving strange objects in the traps, was driving Spider mad.

"I don't think mentioning stealing is a problem," Ninda said. "Topol is an honest man. Eventually people will have to see that. And maybe all of these things people think have been stolen have just been misplaced. After all, nothing very valuable has gone missing."

She was thoughtful for a moment. "Still, it's true that people are slow to give up on outmoded stereotypes. Hmmm." Ninda was just about to ask Spider if he had any ideas for getting around this when the front door burst open. Leo (who had been crouched underneath the grandfather clock) made a break for it. Spider jumped up and dashed after him, nearly knocking the triplets down.

"Why are you home so early?" Ninda asked before rushing outside to help Spider.

"We need a nap," Sassy whispered.

"We're going to be up all night probably," whispered Brick.

"Doing something for someone," whispered Spike, who then turned and winked in the direction Spider had run.

The hair on the back of Ninda's neck stood on end as she ran down the steps after Spider, and it wasn't only from the triplets' whispering and Spike's wink, though she knew they were Up to No Good. What if Leo attacked one of the Rhinnestaadtians?

She chased Spider, who chased Leo right into the center of the camp. There, they both stopped short at an amazing sight. Topol was sitting on a three-legged stool playing a stringed instrument that was no bigger than a ukulele. (Later, upon closer inspection, Ninda decided that the instrument with the black-and-white cow pattern on it *was* a ukulele—but the Rhinnestaadtians had a different name for it.)

The sight of Topol playing music was nothing special—after all, it was one of his favorite things to do, and in the past few days, Ninda and Spider had observed him playing his instrument many times. What was amazing was that Leo was sitting upright next to the giant man, leaning his head against Topol's shins in an adoring fashion.

"Don't move!" Spider called out. "I'll sneak up and grab him before he bites!"

Topol laughed. "Afraid of him I should be?" He continued strumming. "In old country, we call him 'charmkin.' Music we play and follow all the charmkins along behind us wherever we go!"

"Are you sure this is the same kind of animal?" Spider asked cautiously.

"Of course! The stripes of the black and red tell me so."

Spider nodded, remembering that Rhinnestaadt is on the northern tip of the Panjeeyan continent.

"They're very rare," said Spider, wondering if, in fact, that could possibly be the case. For an endangered species there certainly were a lot of Leo's friends causing trouble around Eel-Smack. And yet, here was Leo sitting adoringly, not attackingly, listening to Topol play music.

"So, this is why Leo keeps trying to escape. He wanted to come down here to listen to the music," Spider said.

"Do the charmkins really follow you wherever you go when you play music?" Ninda asked, a brilliant plan forming in her head.

"They are finding the sound of the *grissinet* impossible to resist, always," Topol said.

Leo twined around Topol's ankles, just as a cat, happy to see his owner, would.

Ninda clapped her hands, smiling hugely. "Okay, you and Leo stay right here till I get back. I'm going to go make a phone call," she said, "and Spider, you need to make one, too."

"Who do I need to call?" he asked.

"The Tom Thumb Habitat for Small Endangered Animals!"

August 7,
No Countdown to CRAVE (as I am not certain as to how much longer exactly I must wear a walking cast)

Dear Journal,

Today I received welcome news on several fronts!

Phileas Pogonip telephoned early this morning and confirmed what I suspected all along. Ned A. Paddywhack most certainly did not attend the B. Knighted Academy for Butlers. I shall expose him for the fraud he is!

The other welcome news is that Dr. Hannibal believes I have healed enough that I may receive a walking cast. This will result in my early release from this wretched place.

I intend to take Paddywhack by surprise, arriving by taxi so as not to arouse in him a suspicion that he is about to be turned out of the house. Before resuming my rightful place, I shall deliver a lecture to him regarding the impropriety of claiming credentials that he does not have.

Yet another bright spot came to light after I tested the remote control grime with my thumb.

Television viewers all over Eel-Smack, including myself, were treated to the unusual sight of a boy (Spider) in a trench coat and sunglasses with a squirrel on his shoulder—a squirrel who was not attacking, but just sitting, and a girl (Ninda) in a camouflage jacket and red cap. They were accompanied by a huge man who was playing a cow-patterned musical instrument of some sort. I hadn't the faintest idea as to his identity, nor what his connection to the Bellweathers might be. I peered closely at the set. The children looked well enough. I sighed.

The camera panned out and I could see dozens upon dozens of squirrels following the three. It was as if there was a human-and-animal parade, going right through the middle of the village of Eel-Smack-by-the-Bay.

The large man led everyone to a big van that read Tom Thumb Habitat for Small Endangered Animals on the side. Imagine my joy when the camera showed the man climbing into the van and the little animals swarming up and into the vehicle after him. My problem solved.

Almost.

The doors were shut—and the only squirrel left was the one sitting on Spider's shoulder.

I do not know about that snake Paddywhack, but I am certain that I am capable of dealing with one squirrel. After all, did I not graduate first in my class at the B. Knighted Academy for Butlers? And did I not manage to survive an entire house filled with Endangered Albino Alligators? I am sure he holds no such qualifications.

I looked again. This squirrel had the distinctive red-and-black striping about the head one associates with the Endangered Reticulated Attack Squirrel. However, he possessed something else—the rather tan-colored ears of the species of squirrel more commonly associated with the area in and around Eel-Smack-by-the-Bay. A species which displays an unsavory habit that almost rivals that of the Attack Squirrel. Hmmmm.

The newscaster turned back to the camera.

"And so, as you see here, one brave man and his young friends are ridding the village of Eel-Smack-by-the-Bay of the dangerous beasts that have been threatening our citizens."

What a Relief.

I believe this may be the first time in my long and exemplary career that someone else has cleaned up a mess that I . . . had a hand in making.

No sooner had I breathed a grateful sigh, then Ninda popped up in front of the newscaster. "Vote Topol for mayor!" she said.

The camera cut back to the newscaster who said, "Vote Topol, indeed!"

Really, Paddywhack expected to keep up with Ninda? Ridiculous!

·16·
The Truth of the Matter

"I've always heard that doctors make the worst patients, but I think it safe to say we don't," Dr. Hannibal remarked as he put the last piece of wet plaster onto Benway's new walking cast. "Butlers do."

The hospital staff had decided that Benway had recovered enough (and was sour enough, and was enough of a pain in the neck) that he could be released nearly a week ahead of time.

"I am sure I've no idea what you are talking about," Benway said.

"You may not believe this, Benway," said Dr.

Hannibal, washing the white goo off his hands, "but not all of our patients become so agitated that we have to put them into soft, cushy rooms."

"Certainly there were one or two incidents that may have been misinterpreted," Benway conceded.

"You're free to leave as soon as the cast hardens in about a half an hour." Dr. Hannibal made a note in Benway's chart and then turned to go. He paused in the doorway. "Do us both a favor and try to be very careful. I'll come to the Lighthouse on the Hill in a few weeks to take it off. I think that would be better than you coming here."

When the doctor had gone, the Positively Bothersome Junior Nurse helped Benway collect his belongings and the books that the children had brought for him to read.

"It's going to be boring here without you," she said. "Say, maybe when Dr. Hannibal goes to the Lighthouse on the Hill to take your cast off, I could go with him."

Benway cleared his throat. "Perhaps," he said. "Would you be so kind as to call a taxi for me?"

"Golly, isn't anyone picking you up? That doesn't seem right. Wow, do you think you've been here so long they've forgotten you?" she asked.

Benway sighed. "The taxi, please."

Adams Hackney, the only cab driver in Eel-Smack-by-the-Bay, loaded Benway's belongings into the car. He seemed surprised that Benway was returning to the Lighthouse on the Hill so soon.

"That leg isn't healed all the way yet," he observed after helping Benway hobble the few steps from the hospital to the car. Once his passenger was settled into the backseat, he pulled away from the curb.

"If I was going to stay with that family, I'd want two good legs. You never know when you're going to need to run."

Benway stared steadily out the window.

"I heard the triplets set fire to the place last year," Hackney said.

"The fire was not the triplets' doing," Benway corrected without breaking his gaze. The village rolled by.

"Still, ya never know what's gonna happen there." The cab turned a corner. "That oldest boy and all those dangerous animals. I don't know how you can sleep at night. And that professor. I hear he's always shouting and throwing things. I'd sure be careful." Hackney shook his head.

"I would appreciate a few moments of quiet," Benway said before the other man could go on. They rode the next few blocks in silence.

Halfway up Lighthouse Hill, though, Hackney exclaimed, "What in the world is a circus doing here?"

Benway looked out at the colorful tents dotting the property around the lighthouse. People appeared to be celebrating, and he thought he spotted the huge man he'd seen on television with Ninda and Spider.

"They're Rhinnestaadtians," Benway said. "Would you be so kind as to park here?" he asked, indicating a stretch of driveway partially hidden from the house by one of the tents.

"That's pretty far for you to walk with that leg of yours," the cabbie said. "And if you need to run . . ."

"I won't be walking. Or running, either," Benway

said. "I need you to go up to the house and fetch the fellow who has been filling in for me temporarily. I must speak with him before I see the family. His name is Paddywhack."

Hackney started to protest. "It's an uphill walk! That place is dangerous! What if that Dr. Bellweather is home?" Benway cut him off.

"You must simply be certain to stand very close to the front door after ringing the doorbell. I will, of course, pay you for your extra effort," he said. "Quite a bit."

Benway watched the very reluctant cabdriver walk up toward the Lighthouse on the Hill.

"NO ONE CALLED A TAXI," Spike, Brick, and Sassy screamed in unison when they opened the door to see Hackney.

Thanks to Benway's advice, the cabbie had missed being hit with a box of rubber bands after ringing the doorbell. Confronted with the triplets, he took a step back but then looked up to see the fifth-floor window was still open. Stepping forward again, he said, "I'm here to see Paddywhack."

"PADDYWHACK?" Brick looked at Sassy.

"PADDYWHACK?" Sassy looked at Spike.

"PADDYWHACK?" Spike looked back at Brick.

"WHY?" Brick shouted.

"I, uh, heard he was just filling in for Benway," Hackney said, standing now in the doorway. "See, I just thought I might have another job for him."

The triplets smiled their deceptively innocent smiles.

"DOING WHAT?" Sassy screamed. My, she was loud.

"Um . . . driving a taxi," Hackney replied. "Is he here?"

"HE'S NOT HERE!" screamed Spike.

"IF PADDYWHACK WAS HERE, WE'D BE LOCKED IN A CLOSET!" yelled Sassy.

"Well, that's—"

"PADDYWHACK CAN'T DRIVE!" Brick interrupted.

"HE CAN'T DO ANYTHING!" shrieked Spike.

"Even so—"

"THERE IS NO PADDYWHACK!" they shouted together.

"What?" Hackney, in spite of himself, leaned forward. He wasn't sure he was hearing correctly.

"WE'RE TAKING CARE OF OURSELVES!" yelled Brick.

Sassy stood on her tiptoes and before Hackney could move she shouted in his ear, "IF YOU SEE BENWAY DON'T TELL HIM!!!!"

Hackney got back in the car. He closed his eyes and leaned his head against the headrest for a moment. "They're so loud," he moaned.

"You spoke with the triplets?" Benway asked. "Where is Paddywhack?"

"There is no Paddywhack," the driver said, not looking at Benway.

"Pardon?" The butler's voice was sharp.

"How can you stand it there?" the cabdriver asked. "I was there for five minutes and I may have to take the rest of the day off!"

"What did you say about Paddywhack?" Benway demanded.

"There is no Paddywhack," Hackney repeated,

opening his eyes and turning his head to look at Benway.

"Oh, my! What has the professor done?" Benway gasped. "Throwing things, yes. Shouting, yes. But murder? I simply cannot believe it!"

In spite of his headache, Hackney smiled.

"The professor didn't have anything to do with it. Those three say there never was a Paddywhack. No butler at all, other than you. No one crazy enough to take on that job," he said, and then rummaged around in the glove compartment for aspirin. After locating it he glanced back to see that Benway looked stiff. More so than usual.

"They lied to me again," said Benway quietly.

"Uh, do you want me to take you up the hill?" Hackney asked.

"After all I've done for them."

"I can, but I'm not going anywhere near the front door," the driver said. "I think you're crazy to want to go back there. I didn't even see the rest of the family, but they're just as nuts as the triplets, I hear. Maybe not as loud, but still . . ."

"All my time. All my life."

"So . . . you don't want me to take you up the hill?"

"No, thank you. Drive me back to the village."

It was the first time in anyone's memory that Tristan Benway was seen lunching at Barnacle Bill's Pretty Okay Diner.

Adams Hackney was paid extra to sit five tables away from him and not to speak.

August 9

Dear Journal,

I instructed Adams Hackney to bring me to Barnacle Bill's Pretty Okay Diner. I need time to think. I am completely flummoxed. I have never used that word in relation to myself before. And yet, there it is. I am flummoxed.

As we drove, I considered the worrying I had done over the mistreatment of the triplets. Becoming so agitated on their behalf that I was shut up in the mental ward of hospital!

My anxiety over the state of affairs at the Lighthouse on the Hill kept me from enjoying the first break from domestic service I have had in years, and the family must have seen this.

Still, they lied.

The aggravating knowledge that I have been lied to has been joined by a new and equally uncomfortable thought.

Is it possible that the Bellweather family does not need me?

I was so concerned that they couldn't take care of themselves when in reality they were doing just that.

Spider cleared up the squirrel mess . . . his mess and mine, with no help from me whatsoever.

Ninda rescued the Rhinnestaadtians. Surely a girl who is capable of caring for an entire group of displaced persons is capable of caring for herself.

The triplets are obviously just as capable of getting themselves out of trouble as they are getting themselves into trouble.

I certainly had not needed to run the household from my hospital bed. In fact, the whole family has proved Quite Capable of caring for themselves. They managed to do this as well as visit me; bringing "snacks" and books and paint samples for me to look at.

Have I been wrong about who is caring for whom? This is a train of thought that is Most Uncomfortable.

I was grateful to give up this line of thinking when we finally arrived at Barnacle Bill's Pretty Okay Diner. I ordered tea and instructed Adams Hackney to sit as far from me as possible.

The tabletop is sticky, as I had known it would be. The waitress and the cook have very loud voices and the sound of their conversation will not be helpful to my state of mind as I contemplate my future. Still, as I am not in the habit of coming here, my whereabouts are unlikely to be discovered before I have had a chance to consider what I should do next. Not that anyone will come looking for me.

Why should the family look for me when they don't need me?

It is just something that would have been nice, that's all.

Hmph!

Well, I imagine they can continue to get along just fine without me. Perhaps it is time to dust off my dream of a little cottage Far, Far Away. I could have a flower garden of my own. One that is not full of holes dug by the triplets. I'm sure it would be very beautiful, if very flat. (Although, come to think of it, a garden full of holes could be interesting to look at.)

At the B. Knighted Academy for Butlers, we are trained to maintain a professional distance. I somehow lost sight of that, but I recognize once again the importance of that training. In all good conscience I cannot stay with the Bellweathers if they do not need me.

• 17 •

Wrapping It Up

"No need to heat up that pot roast," the waitress called to the cook at Barnacle Bill's Pretty Okay Diner.

"Eh? Thaddeus Bohack'll be coming in and wanting his lunch soon," the cook said, and then mumbled something about people who ordered the same lunch every day of their lives.

"No, hon. I ran into him on my way to work," the waitress said. "Says he finally has the goods on that kid. Bohack's taking him to St. Whiplash's, so he's gonna miss lunch."

Benway's cup clattered to its saucer. "Check, please!"

he choked out. He shut his journal and got to his feet very quickly for someone with a broken leg.

After a short taxi ride, Benway arrived at the lighthouse on the heels of three very angry men. Phrases like "When I get my hands on those little so-and-so's" and "This is the last straw" issued from their furious lips. By the time Adams Hackney unloaded the luggage, the butler had hobbled up to the porch before one of the three could ring the doorbell.

"May I help you, gentlemen?" Benway asked.

"Where are those three?" shouted Dr. Dume, shaking a thermos Benway recognized as being from the Bellweather pantry.

"Tell that Spider to pack a toothbrush," Bohack snarled.

"Get Ninda and that Rhinnestaadtian out here, too!" growled Ex-Mayor Scrunchmunnie.

"I most certainly will not," said Benway.

"Fine, I'll do it myself," said the ex-mayor, ringing the doorbell. At the sound of the foghorn Benway and Bohack pressed their bodies up against the door. Scrunchmunnie and Dr. Dume looked at them curiously. Adams Hackney deposited Benway's bag on the porch then scurried away. Nothing fell from above.

The door opened and three curly blond heads popped out. The triplets' deceptively innocent blue eyes widened when they saw Dr. Dume, the thermos he held, and the terrible expression on his face.

"HI, DR. DUME!" Sassy shouted.

"NICE TO SEE YOU!" yelled Brick.

"GOTTA RUN!" screamed Spike.

The three pushed out the door and past the startled paleontologist before jumping off the porch and disappearing into the Rhinnestaadtian celebration that was happening on the lawn.

Dr. Dume ran after them. Benway shook his head. One thing at a time.

Meanwhile, Dr. Bellweather was having a miserable morning, just the latest in a series. There was a very loud celebration happening out on the front lawn; Topol had evidently won the election. It was to be hoped the Rhinnestaadtians would move to their new home quickly.

Earlier Dr. Bellweather had opened the window and shouted, but no one could hear him over the din. A little later, the foghorn blared, but all he had on hand to throw was a box of rubber bands, which would hardly make an impression. He didn't even bother to look to see if he'd hit his mark.

His stomach grumbled but he couldn't eat the exotic dishes that smelled so wonderful—they were spicy and upset his stomach. He was starving, and to top it all off, he couldn't find the old metal ice-cube tray he thought he'd laid on the table just last night. The tiny compartments were perfect for holding little springs and screws, and now those bits were scattered all over his workspace. It seemed that nothing in his lab would stay put. A few days previously his mining invention had gone missing, but it turned up later, right where he'd thought he'd left it.

Benway wasn't around to "tidy" the lab and lose things. The aggravating fact was that Dr. Bellweather had no one to blame but himself. Drat!

The truth was . . . Eugene Bellweather, PhD, was realizing that Benway had been of some use. The butler provided a veneer (even if it was just illusion) of some order to the Lighthouse on the Hill. Meals were on time, the doorbell was answered. True, the children were *always* disruptive . . . but, somehow, they seemed a little less so when Benway was in residence.

When the foghorn blared again he stomped down the stairs, roaring as he always did, but it sounded a little hollow. He got to the bottom step and was startled to hear a very welcome voice telling whomever it was that he'd have to see if the master of the house was in.

Dr. Bellweather stepped into the front hall. "What do you mean by coming in here and disturbing my concentration?" he shouted. Thaddeus Bohack and ex-Mayor Scrunchmunnie glared back at him. Benway, wearing a walking cast, turned to look at the professor.

"The gentlemen are here to see you, sir," he said. "I knew you were busy, and I was about to ask them to come back later."

"I'm not returning! Spider can come with me now, or Sheriff Omar will pick him up later–but he's being charged with harboring Attack Squirrels."

"And your daughter is being charged with voter fraud!" Scrunchmunnie snarled.

They were interrupted by the sight of Leo the squirrel dragging an ice-cube tray across the front hall, in what had to be the best case of worst timing ever.

"Ack! See? I knew he was guilty–this just proves it!" Bohack said, pointing. "We'll see how much Spider likes animals once he's in reform school because of 'em!"

"Are you threatening my son?" Dr. Bellweather shouted, his eyebrows assuming a karate stance.

"Sir, if I may?" Benway asked, then turned to the dogcatcher. "Why are you threatening to take an innocent child to a reform school?" he asked.

"Innocent, nothing," Bohack spat. "I have proof he brought these here Attack Squirrels to town!"

"Attack Squirrels?" Benway asked. Leo was trying (unsuccessfully) to shove the ice-cube tray through the cracked-open front door.

Benway tsked. "It is not my place to offer an opinion, but if it were, I certainly would have expected a professional to know the difference between an Attack

Squirrel and a Thieving Squirrel." There was a gasp from behind the grandfather clock. All heads turned toward the timepiece. Spider sheepishly stepped out.

Bohack glared and Benway stooped to pick up the squirrel and the ice-cube tray. "Anyone can see by the tan ears of this one that they are different species. This particular group of squirrels has long been a plague to Eel-Smack-by-the-Bay. I can assure you that Spider did not bring *Thieving* Squirrels here!"

"Er . . . of course not!" the professor said.

Benway grasped Leo with one hand and pulled the ice-cube tray from him. The squirrel struggled, but Benway fixed him with his patented superior-butler look, and the animal gave up.

Just then Ninda burst through the front door, her face flushed.

"Mayor Topol told me he thought he'd seen you come in here!" she said.

"Mayor Topol?" Scrunchmunnie snarled. "I have news for you, little lady! You're guilty of Voter Fraud with a capital VF! That washed-up king-of-a-small-country-no-one-cares-about isn't even a citizen!"

Scrunchmunnie smiled a mean smile. "He can't be elected mayor—and the fact that you tried to get him elected means you're in big trouble!" Ninda looked a little worried.

Benway limped over to his bag. He pulled out the book she had lent him in the hospital. He opened it and read:

Eel-Smack-by-the-Bay Village Charter

November 8, 1722

Any individual, regardless of country of origin, or time spent here in this country, may be eligible to fill the mayoral post of his village.

Benway looked up from the book.

"With all due respect, sir, had you bothered to learn your history, you would know that Eel-Smack was first settled before this country was established. No one was a citizen and, therefore, anyone might hold a government position. The charter was never updated, meaning that Anyone may run for mayor."

There was no mistaking the triumph on Ninda's face, or the purple outrage on the ex-mayor's.

"According to the by-laws of Eel-Smack-by-the-Bay, you must vacate the mayoral mansion immediately," Ninda said. Scrunchmunnie's face became even more purple as she went on. "Mayor Topol kindly agreed to remain our guest until tomorrow night so that you could have time to remove your belongings."

The ex-mayor began to sputter, and Benway stepped forward to take things further in hand. "Now, if you'll excuse us," he turned sideways and made the universal "scram" gesture with his head, somehow managing to look dignified as he did so. "I believe Dr. Bellweather was on the brink of an important discovery and must get back to it."

Tucking Leo the Thieving Squirrel underneath his arm, Benway opened the door.

"Since your accusations are groundless, and good science will bear this out"—this last directed at Bohack, who was as speechless as the ex-mayor was sputtering—"I suggest you leave. Good day."

The professor stared at Benway. Neither Bohack

nor Scrunchmunnie offered the slightest argument to Benway. Almost reeling, they stumbled through the door. Perhaps getting people to leave was a skill one possessed naturally from having been first in his class at the B. Knighted Academy for Butlers.

The two slammed out the door, leaving Spider, Ninda, and even Dr. Bellweather gazing in awe at Benway, who made himself busy putting the books back into his luggage.

Finally Spider asked, "Benway–is that true? How could I have missed that?" He seemed shocked at his own ignorance. "And say, how did you know about Thieving Squirrels?"

"I received quite an education while I was in the hospital, and I put two and two together. Eel-Smack-by-the-Bay is hardly a haven for criminal types, and when I learned of these squirrels and their delight in theft, it all made sense to me," Benway said, zipping shut a compartment in his suitcase and looking pleased with himself. He smiled down at Spider. "Don't feel too awful about it. Even experts would be fooled by the incredible similarity."

"I was so sure he was an Attack Squirrel," Spider said. "Um . . . I did have something to do with bringing those here. I thought they were endangered. . . ." There was a very uncharacteristic look on Benway's face. An almost guilty one.

"About the squirrels, boy," he said. "I need to tell you that–" Spider looked up just in time to see the strange look on Benway's face flee.

"Er . . . my theory is that the Thieving Squirrels and the Attack Squirrels have gotten together. Their differing strengths have combined to make a stronger species," Benway said, Omitting Some Information.

The notion of squirrel evolution excited Spider so much that he forgot all about the odd look that had crossed Benway's features. "And now there's a whole new species of super squirrel! Hurray for diversity!" Spider exclaimed, just as the triplets slammed through the front door.

Mrs. Bellweather came out from Benway's quarters, a paintbrush in her hand.

"What a surprise! Welcome home, dear!" she said to him.

Sassy yawned. Hugely. "WELL, WE'RE GOING TO TAKE A NAP!" she shrieked.

"DON'T WORRY! WE'LL PUT IT BACK WHEN WE'RE THROUGH!" Brick cackled.

Before they could escape to the safety of their seventh-floor art studio, the foghorn blared.

"DON'T!" they yelled in unison, but it was too late. Benway opened the door to Dr. Dume. The triplets froze in place. They weren't scared . . . exactly.

Dr. Dume shook the thermos at them. "You three are in big trouble! I found this underneath the fossil I just excavated! No one else eats applesauce and beets!"

"Am I to take it that the triplets had something to do with your recent 'amazing discovery'?" Dr. Bellweather asked.

"Yes! Those three juvenile delinquents tampered with my excavation! There is no Dumeasaur!" He looked down at the thermos, shook his head as though he could not believe such an ordinary object spelled the end of his dreams of a Big Scientific Find, and then looked up again.

"I'm suing! And once the judge gets a load of those

three, he'll probably lock them up and throw away the key!"

"Suing?" roared the professor, his eyebrows springing to life. Mrs. Bellweather merely shrugged. People were always threatening to sue her family.

"Sir, if I may?" Benway asked, turning to the triplets. His tone was severe. "Did you three tamper with this man's excavation?"

"WE THOUGHT WE WERE HELPING!" shouted Sassy.

"DR. DUME SEEMED SO STRESSED!" screamed Brick.

"WE JUST WANTED TO PUT OUR FIND WHERE HE COULD FIND IT!" yelled Spike.

"Dear, dear," Benway said. "And to think that your little action will cost this man his career!"

"What?" gasped Dume "These three are the ones in trouble! Why should my career be in danger?"

"Dr. Bellweather, wouldn't you imagine that when the news is out that Dr. Dume was taken in by the work of three ten-year-olds, it might be difficult for him to work as a scientist?" Benway said. "Why, he'll be the laughingstock of the scientific community." Dr. Bellweather nodded.

Benway held out his hand for the thermos. "Well . . . should you need a career change, I know of a very good academy for butlers." He paused for dramatic effect. "It seems a shame that this has to get out at all. After all . . . if no one were to discover that you were so easily fooled by mere children, you'd likely be able to keep your career."

The whole family watched the scientist's face. It was obvious that a battle to do what was right raged inside him. It ended with him choosing to do the wrong thing for science—but the right thing for himself.

"Fine." He ground out the word. "But don't ever let me see you at a science camp again!" He pointed a shaking finger at the triplets and fumbled with his other hand for the door handle behind him. "Or, so help me, I'll bring you up on charges of engineering a hoax, even if it means watching my career go up in flames!"

He left, slamming the door behind him.

Benway was the first to speak when Dume had gone. "My, but *he* was dramatic!"

"No more science camp for us," whispered Brick.

"We'll have to think of something else to get the world to Sit Up and Take Notice," whispered Sassy.

"Benway, what do you think of opera?" whispered Spike.

"What a question," Benway said. He and the rest of the family smoothed down the hair on the backs of their necks. "What does Paddywhack think?" he frowned.

Mrs. Bellweather stepped forward. "Oh, Benway, dear. We're so sorry we deceived you. We truly thought it was in your best interest. There is no Paddywhack."

Benway held up a hand. "Say no more about it," he said. "I knew there was no Paddywhack."

The family stared.

"I knew the whole time," Benway repeated, grasping the handle of his suitcase. "I must go unpack."

"And I'm going back to work," Dr. Bellweather said, heading up the stairs. On the second step, he cleared his throat and turned around. "Welcome home, Benway."

August 10

Dear Journal,

What a fascinating end to the day.

This evening, after the children had gone to bed (one hopes), Professor Bellweather came to my quarters. (Which Lillian Bellweather painted white in my absence. I was . . . tickled pink, as the saying goes.)

I was surprised to see the professor standing in my doorway. This is not something he often does. In fact, I cannot recall a single instance of it happening before.

"Is there something you wish for me to do?" I asked. He cleared his throat, and then said, "No."

I could not be rude and ask him what he was doing there, so we simply sat for a few moments.

"Er . . . is there anything I can do for you?" he finally asked.

Journal, it is a Very Good thing that I was seated, or I might have fallen right over.

"I don't believe so," I said.

He looked around my room—it is a suite really, my bed in one room, my desk and two chairs in the other. Plain and uncluttered.

"Do you have everything you need?" he asked.

"Indeed, I do," I replied.

"How is the leg?" he asked.

I am not one to complain—though it does ache a bit still.

"Jolly good," I said, really wondering now.

"Good, good," he said. "Would you . . . like a television set in here?" he asked.

"Lord, no!" I said. "I would never watch it." Dangerous devices those are.

We sat for a few more minutes.

After a long silence, he stood to leave. When he got to the door, he suddenly turned back to look at me.

"Thank you, Benway, for everything," he said,

and I realized anew that the Bellweather family cannot get on without me.

I also discovered that as much as they need me, I need them.

I need them.

How extraordinary.

True, they deceived me . . . but I deceived them as well. As the triplets would say, "That makes us even."

Well, dear Journal. Having a break wasn't nearly as nice as I thought it would be—but being appreciated certainly is.

It would appear that Dr. Bellweather has finally learned to appreciate my impeccable service to his family. He has pledged to spare me his little displays of temper from now on. I believe he will keep that promise.

For at least a little while.

THE END

ACKNOWLEDGMENTS

People should always be cautious when they go poking around an acknowledgment page in the hope of seeing their names. Most authors, while very grateful, are not that organized. This translates into forgetting to thank certain people who were critical to the success of a project. Which in turn leads to hurt feelings and resolution on the part of the forgettee to never help the forgetter again. Which is a bad thing. If you are a person who so much as held the door open for me while I was working on this book, consider yourself thanked and please look no further. Oh, and if I mentioned your name in the acknowledgments for *Leaving the Bellweathers*, consider yourself thanked again. But don't get greedy about seeing your name in print.

That said, a special thanks to my beloveds–Steve, Johnathon, Max, and Chelsea Venuti. Thank you, Emma Kolb Price, for practically raising Chelsea while I finished this one. Thank you, Kim Turrisi and SCBWI–especially the Nevada Chapter. As always, thanks go to the amazing Tracey Adams of Adams Literary. Thank you as well, you fine folk at Egmont USA, including (but not limited to) my editor Regina Griffin, Alison S. Weiss, Elizabeth (Lawsy) Law, Doug Pocock, Nico Medina, Mary Albi, and Rob Guzman. Finally, a heartfelt thanks goes to the members of my writing family for listening to the first chapters of *The Butler Gets a Break* and for babysitting me throughout the process: Emma Dryden, Jim Averbeck, Michele Veillon, Ellen Hopkins, and Susan Hart Lindquist. Extra kisses to Susan for allowing me to practically live with her in the Cedarville house while I wrote and revised. And to Prudence Choi, for the use of her deck.

I am grateful to all for everything.

KRISTIN CLARK VENUTI's first novel, *Leaving the Bellweathers*, introduced the world to a family of remarkable characters and received an E.B. White Read Aloud Honor. A children's-theater producer, scene painter, and two-time black belt, she lives in the Santa Cruz Mountains of California with her husband and children. You can visit her online at www.leavingthebellweathers.com.